CU01507309

CHAPTER 1 THE CALL TO DUTY

It was a crisp fall morning when Sergeant Nathan Walker stood before a group of young recruits, their faces a mixture of fear and excitement. The drill sergeant's voice cut through the early morning air like a blade.

"Alright, listen up! This isn't your mama's house. We're not here to coddle you. You're going to sweat, you're going to bleed, and you're going to question every single decision you've made in your life that led you here. But by the end of this, you'll be a soldier. Do you hear me?"

"Yes, Sergeant!" they yelled in unison.

Nathan, only 26 years old but already an experienced combat veteran, had been assigned to oversee these recruits. He'd been through the hell of boot camp and the harsh realities of war, but this moment was different. Standing here, watching these young men and women, some barely old enough to vote, made him reflect on his own journey.

ECHOS OF VALOUR

GEORGE RICHARDSON
Copyright © 2025 George Richardson

DEDICATION

To all members of the armed forces, past and present, around the world you have stood as shields in times of conflict, as beacons in moments of uncertainty,demonstrating the highest virtues of service, sacrifice, and unity.

It is with deep respect and gratitude that this book is dedicated to your enduring legacy a tribute to the lives you've touched, the freedoms you've defended, and the brotherhood and sisterhood that transcend borders and time.

ACKNOWLEDGMENTS

To my beloved wife, Kerry your unwavering love and constant encouragement have been the foundation of everything I do. Through every challenge, every moment of doubt, and every burst of inspiration, you've stood by me with grace and patience. Your belief in me has been a guiding light, and your strength has carried me through the moments I couldn't carry myself. The countless hours you've spent listening to my ideas, offering your insights, and reminding me of the importance of this journey have shaped this book in ways I can't fully express.

Thank you for being my sounding board, my partner, and my greatest supporter. This book is a reflection of not only my passion but also the love and inspiration you've provided me every day. You are my muse, my greatest treasure, and I am forever grateful for you. Every word written in these pages is a testament to you.

He remembered his first day in uniform, the same uncertainty mixed with hope. That hope had slowly faded

over the years, replaced by a cold, pragmatic sense of duty. It wasn't about idealism anymore; it was about survival.

He looked out over the group. Among them was Private James Monroe, a tall, lanky kid from a small town, looking like he'd never seen the business end of a rifle. Then there was Lieutenant Sarah Callahan, a young officer with a sharp mind and an even sharper tongue, who had joined for reasons Nathan didn't quite understand yet. And finally, Private First Class Marco Rivera, who seemed too old to be here, his tired eyes betraying a past he wasn't eager to share.

The first day was always the hardest. They were thrown into a rigorous regimen: running, pushups, sit-ups, the works. The heat bore down on them like a hammer, and sweat streamed down their faces, but the only thing that mattered was keeping up.

"Move it! Move it!" shouted Sergeant Walker as he jogged past them, his voice a relentless force. "You think the enemy's going to wait for you to catch your breath? We don't stop! Not here, not ever!"

James struggled to keep pace. His legs were burning, his chest tight. He wasn't used to this kind of physical strain.

He had joined the army because he thought it would be an adventure, a chance to prove himself. But this was nothing like the daydreams of glory he had imagined.

Lieutenant Callahan, however, was already out in front, her uniform immaculate, her posture perfect. She was fast, faster than Nathan had expected from someone so new. He had heard she came from a family with a military history, and it seemed that her legacy had shaped her determination.

Marco, on the other hand, lagged behind. Nathan kept an eye on him, sensing that the older man was struggling.

There was something off about the way he moved; his joints creaked, and he winced every time he pushed harder. Nathan made a mental note to check on him after the workout.

As the morning training session continued, the recruits pushed themselves harder, their bodies beginning to protest. The drill sergeant's relentless voice kept them moving, never allowing them a moment of respite.

"Focus!" Nathan barked as he observed James stumbling again, his feet unsteady. "This isn't just about physical strength, it's about your will to fight through the pain. The enemy doesn't care if you're tired. You think you're the only one exhausted out here? Everyone's feeling it, but it's those who keep moving that survive."

James gritted his teeth and tried to keep up, but his body was betraying him. Sweat dripped from his forehead, and his breath was ragged. He pushed his legs harder, though every step felt heavier than the last. He couldn't shake the feeling that he was already failing, and that thought gnawed at him, like a wolf circling its prey.

Meanwhile, Lieutenant Callahan was a force to be reckoned with. Her pace was steady, unwavering. Nathan could see the discipline in her eyes, a fierce determination that told him she wasn't just here to follow orders, she was here to command. He couldn't help but respect that.

But his attention soon shifted to Marco. The older man had slowed to a near crawl, his face pale and drawn. Nathan jogged over to him, his boots thudding against the dirt as he moved.

"Private Rivera," Nathan called, his tone quieter but still commanding. "You good?"

Marco's gaze was unfocused, his breathing shallow. He gave a weak nod but didn't say anything.

Nathan's eyes narrowed. He wasn't buying it. "You're not keeping up, Rivera. What's going on?"

The older man hesitated for a moment, then let out a heavy sigh, his shoulders sagging. "Just… just tired, Sergeant. I'm not as young as I used to be."

Nathan wasn't convinced. The man was older, sure, but that didn't explain the way he was moving, like every step was an effort. The veteran sergeant glanced around. The rest of the recruits were pushing themselves, some struggling, but they were still moving forward. Marco, however, was flagging.

"You're not fooling me," Nathan said firmly. "You're not going to quit on me, Private. You're going to finish this workout, even if I have to drag you across the finish line."

Marco's tired eyes met his for a brief second, and for a moment, Nathan saw something dark flicker behind them, something that suggested there was more to this man's struggle than just physical exhaustion.

But before Marco could respond, a loud voice cut through the air.

"Walker!" It was Captain Reynolds, the base's commanding officer, and he was heading toward them with purpose. "You've got five minutes to get those recruits in line for the next phase of training. "Don't waste time, Sergeant."

Nathan gave Marco one last look before turning to the rest of the group. "Alright, you heard the Captain! Move your asses, now!"

The recruits started jogging forward again, the drill sergeant at their heels, but the tension between him and Marco lingered in the back of his mind. Whatever was going on with Rivera, Nathan had a feeling it wasn't just physical fatigue.

As they moved into the next phase of training, Nathan kept his eyes on his recruits, determined to push them to their limits, but even more determined to find out what was really going on with Marco.

The next phase of training was a brutal test of endurance and teamwork. The recruits were split into pairs, tasked with carrying heavy sandbags from one end of the training field to the other.

The sun had climbed higher, its heat more oppressive now, and sweat poured from every pore. Nathan could see the exhaustion written across every face, but he wasn't going to let up.

"Team up! Move! Move!" he barked, urging them into position. "This isn't about doing it alone. You rely on your partner, or you fail together!"

James, still gasping for breath, stumbled toward the nearest recruit, a broad shouldered kid named Eric. They paired off quickly, and Nathan watched as they struggled to lift the heavy bag, their movements clumsy, their bodies still trying to recover from the morning's run.

Lieutenant Callahan, unsurprisingly, was already ahead. She had teamed up with another recruit, and they moved with synchronised precision, their sandbags barely slowing them down as they sprinted across the field. Nathan couldn't help but watch her for a moment, her posture perfect, her focus unwavering. There was something about her, something that reminded him of himself when he was younger. It was both admirable and, in a way, frustrating.

Nathan's attention shifted back to Marco, who was struggling to even lift the sandbag.

His face was pale, his movements sluggish. He was still pushing himself, but it

was obvious that every step cost him more than it did the others. Nathan jogged over to him, this time with more purpose.

"Rivera," he called again, his voice low but commanding. "This isn't just about muscles.

11

It's about grit. You think you're the only one feeling pain right now? You think the enemy will care if you're 'too old' to keep going?"

Marco's eyes flickered towards Nathan, a mixture of embarrassment and frustration on his face. "I'm not weak, Sergeant. Just… just need a moment."

Nathan wasn't buying it. "You've got ten seconds. Either you start carrying that weight, or I'll take it from you and carry it myself. Which do you prefer?"

Marco's eyes darkened, a flash of something stubbornness, maybe, passing through them. He nodded, clenched his jaw, and with a grunt, hoisted the sandbag onto his shoulders. The effort was clearly painful, but he didn't drop it. Nathan gave him a sharp nod of approval.

"That's it," Nathan said gruffly. "No more excuses. You're a soldier now, Rivera. Act like it."

As the recruits continued, Nathan kept his eye on the group. James was struggling but working through it. His partner Eric encouraged him along. Callahan was already finishing her second lap, her confidence unshaken. But Marco? The older man's pace had slowed again, and Nathan could tell the sandbag was starting to get the better of him. Each step seemed like a battle, his legs stiff, his back hunched.

By the time the exercise was over, the recruits were covered in dirt and sweat, their faces a portrait of exhaustion. Nathan could feel his own body protesting, but he knew that if they were going to make it through the day, he couldn't show weakness. Not now.

"Alright, take a five minute break," Nathan called. "Hydrate. Catch your breath. But don't think you're done. We've got a long way to go."

The recruits scattered, some sitting on the ground, others leaning against the training equipment. Nathan walked over to a nearby bench, wiped the sweat from his brow, and took a long swig from his canteen. He was lost in thought, his mind turning over the events of the morning.

He glanced at Marco, who had collapsed against a wall, his eyes closed and his chest heaving. There was something about the man that wasn't adding up, something deeper than just a physical struggle. The tension he'd noticed earlier was still there. And Nathan didn't believe it was just fatigue.

He needed answers, but now wasn't the time. The recruits would be back in motion soon, and the next phase of training would demand even more of them. Nathan's gaze flickered towards Lieutenant Callahan, still standing tall, never resting, never letting up. She had a fire in her that was both admirable and, in a way, intimidating.

He couldn't afford to lose anyone not James, not Marco, and certainly not Callahan.

"Back in five!" Nathan shouted, shaking off the thoughts. There will be time to dig deeper into Marco's story later. For now, the next challenge was already on the horizon, and the recruits had no choice but to face it head on.

As the recruits began to move again, Nathan surveyed them, watching for any signs of weakness. The rest of the day was only going to get harder, and he needed to see who would rise to the occasion and who would falter.

The sun was climbing higher, and the real test was just beginning.

The break was short, too short for some of the recruits to recover fully, but Nathan wasn't about to let them slack off.

He could see the weariness in their eyes, the pain in their muscles, but that wasn't going to stop him from pushing them even harder. Boot camp wasn't supposed to be comfortable; it was supposed to be a crucible that forged them into soldiers. And he wasn't about to let any of them off easy.

"Alright, listen up!" Nathan shouted as the recruits began to shuffle back into position, their shoulders sagging with exhaustion. "This next exercise is going to test your mental toughness.

You'll face an obstacle course, tightrope walks, cargo nets, wall climbs, the works. There's no time to think about your aches or your pains. The only thing that matters is finishing."

He paused for a moment, letting the words sink in. Nathan knew the course would push them to their limits, especially after the morning's gruelling workout. Some of them were ready for this kind of challenge, but others were going to struggle. And he wasn't going to go easy on anyone.

"Private Monroe," he called, spotting James near the back of the group, still wiping sweat from his face

. "I know you're still trying to catch your breath from the last round. But if you don't pick it up on this course, you'll be a liability. You hear me?"

James gave him a shaky nod, his breath still coming in ragged gasps. Nathan wasn't sure if the kid was going to make it, but he wasn't about to let him quit. He had to believe that deep down, everyone had the strength to keep going, even when they thought they didn't.

"Lieutenant Callahan," Nathan said next, turning his attention to her. She was already in position, her expression Stoic, ready for the next challenge. "I expect you to lead by example. Stay sharp. Stay focused."

"Yes, Sergeant," Callahan replied, her voice firm but not arrogant. Nathan gave her a quick nod. At least she wasn't going to let him down.

Then, his eyes went back to Marco. The older man was sitting off to the side, his back pressed against a tree. He hadn't gotten up yet, and Nathan could see the stiffness in his movements as he slowly straightened his back.

Marco was exhausted, more than anyone else. But something in Nathan's gut told him there was more to it.

He couldn't put his finger on it yet, but he wasn't letting Marco slip through the cracks.

If the guy was going to make it, he had to dig deep, and Nathan needed to make sure he did.

"Rivera!" Nathan barked, his voice sharp. Marco didn't flinch, but he did slowly get to his feet, his face a mask of determination.

"I'm good, Sergeant," Marco said, though his voice was strained. He was trying to mask it, but Nathan saw through the façade.

"You're not good," Nathan replied, his eyes narrowing. "You're not good until you've finished this course. And if you need help, you better ask for it before you drop. Understood?"

Marco gave a short nod. "Understood."

Nathan wasn't satisfied with that answer, but he couldn't force the man to open up right then. He'd have to check on him later, after the course. Right now, the recruits need to focus.

"Alright, everyone!" Nathan called, his voice booming. "Obstacle course in ten! Get ready.

This is where you separate the men from the boys."

17

He watched as the recruits formed lines, each of them exhausted but trying to hide it. The course stretched out ahead of them: a series of low walls, rope climbs, narrow ledges to balance on, and a muddy pit they'd have to crawl through. The heat of the day was unforgiving, and the scent of sweat and dust mixed with the faint odour of the wet earth in the pit.

"Monroe, you're first," Nathan ordered. He could see the hesitation in the young man's eyes, but he wasn't about to give him a choice. "Move!"

James stumbled forward, wincing as he approached the first obstacle: a low wall. He barely made it over, his hands slipping on the rough surface. Nathan could see the kid was struggling, his movements awkward, but he wasn't giving up.

Callahan was next. She made the first wall look easy, vaulting over it with the kind of fluidity Nathan expected. Her eyes were locked forward, her pace unbroken, as she took on the rope climb like it was nothing.

She was far ahead now, already on the second wall, while James was still fighting on the ropes.

Then came Marco. His movements were slow, deliberate. When he reached the first wall, he hesitated, clearly unsure if his body could handle the strain. Nathan was watching him carefully now, waiting to see if he would falter.

"Come on, Rivera," Nathan muttered under his breath. "You've got this."

Marco stepped up to the wall and, with a grunt, placed one hand on the rough surface. His face twisted with effort, and for a moment, it looked like he might collapse. But then, in an unexpected move, he shoved himself up with one last burst of strength and swung his leg over.

Nathan let out a silent breath of relief. It wasn't graceful, but it was determination. Marco wasn't quitting, not yet.

But as they moved forward along the course, Marco's pace slowed again. Nathan kept his distance, keeping a sharp eye on the older man.

Marco wasn't moving as fast as the others, and there was a distinct limp to his step now.

By the time they reached the final obstacle, the muddy pit, Marco was gasping for air.

He had slowed so much that the rest of the recruits were already waiting for him. James was covered in sweat and dirt, but he had made it through the course with minimal struggle. Callahan had already finished and was waiting at the finish line, her posture still as perfect as when she started.

Nathan stood at the edge of the pit, watching Marco with a critical eye.

"Come on, Rivera," Nathan called again, his voice firm but not unkind. "Finish it. You're not done until you crawl through this mud."

Marco hesitated for a moment, his eyes locking with Nathan's. Then, with a defiant grunt, he dropped to his knees and began crawling through the pit. It was slow, torturous, but he kept moving. Each inch was a battle, but he didn't stop.

When Marco finally emerged from the mud, his face caked in grime, Nathan nodded in approval.

"You finished, Private," he said, his voice low but proud. "That's what matters."

Marco met his gaze for a long moment, his eyes tired but resolute. "I'm not quitting, Sergeant."

Nathan gave him a sharp nod. "I know. Now go join the others."

As Marco trudged toward the rest of the recruits, Nathan turned to the others, his eyes scanning the group. They were all worn out, but they had completed the course. They survived.

And Nathan knew this was only the beginning. There would be more obstacles ahead, physical, mental, and emotional.

But if they could make it through today, there was hope. Hope that maybe, just maybe, they could all become the soldiers they needed to be.

CHAPTER 2 INTO THE UNKNOWN

As the days passed, the intensity of the training only increased. By the end of the second week, the recruits were exhausted, physically and mentally. But Nathan could see the change. They were beginning to come together as a team.

One evening, after the day's drills, they gathered in a small mess hall. The food was bland, the conversation sparse. Nathan watched as James picked at his tray, clearly homesick.

"You alright, kid?" Nathan asked, sitting down across from him.

James looked up, forcing a smile. "Yeah, just… thinking. This isn't what I expected."

"None of it is," Nathan replied quietly. "But it's about what comes after. It's about getting through it. One day at a time."

Weeks of gruelling training wore on, and the recruits were starting to find their rhythm. The endless drills, the harsh words from their sergeants, and the constant physical exhaustion were beginning to shape them into something more than just individuals.

They were becoming a team, a unit, a force to be reckoned with.

Nathan watched the transformation closely. James had improved significantly, though his lanky frame still looked out of place on the field. His speed had increased, and his focus sharpened.

He was no longer the kid who struggled to keep up; he was the kid who now pushed others to do better.

Lieutenant Callahan, true to her nature, led by example. She was always at the front of every formation, whether it was running drills or teaching tactics. Despite her cold exterior, Nathan could tell she had a deep sense of responsibility, she cared about every recruit, even if she didn't always show it.

And Marco... Marco was a mystery. The older man had taken a different approach to training. He wasn't as fast as the others, but he was steady. His experience showed in the way he moved, deliberately and cautiously, as though every step was calculated.

Nathan saw the wear and tear of years on his face, and though Marco never complained,

Nathan knew that some of the physical strain was catching up with him.

One night, after a particularly brutal day of training, Nathan called the group together around the campfire.

"Alright, listen up," Nathan started, his voice commanding. "I know you're all tired, and I know some of you are questioning why you're even here. But let me tell you something. You've all got potential. You wouldn't be here if you didn't.

This isn't just about physical strength, it's about mental toughness. You've all got the mental chops to make it, and that's what's going to keep you going when things get tough. Understand?"

They all nodded, but it was Marco who spoke up. His gravelly voice was surprisingly calm.

"Is it going to get tougher than this, Sergeant?"

Nathan chuckled. "You're damn right, it is. But that's why we do it. You push your limits. You get knocked down, but you get back up. And that's what makes a soldier. You just have to remember that it's not just about you anymore. It's about the guy next to you, the guy who's got your back."

Marco looked around at the group, his tired eyes catching the others' gazes. "I got it. We're in this together."

Nathan gave Marco a nod of approval. "Exactly. You're only as strong as the team around you. And trust me, when you've got a solid unit, there's nothing that can break you."

The fire crackled, the warmth of the flames casting long shadows over the group. The recruits sat in silence for a moment, each processing the weight of Nathan's words.

James was the first to break the quiet. "I didn't realise it until now, but we really are a team. Not just a group of people thrown together."

"That's right, kid," Nathan said, his voice softening just a bit. "You're more than that now. You're a unit. And that means you fight for each other. Don't forget that."

Lieutenant Callahan, who had been watching from the edge of the group, finally spoke up. "What Sergeant Barris is saying is true. You won't get through this alone. And we won't leave anyone behind. Remember that."

Her eyes flicked to Marco, and for a brief moment, her cold exterior seemed to crack.

Nathan could see it, though none of the recruits likely would have noticed: the unspoken understanding between Callahan and Marco, both of them aware of the sacrifice and pain it took to get to this point.

The crackling of the fire seemed to punctuate the silence as the recruits sat a little taller, the weight of their shared purpose settling over them. This wasn't just about surviving the training anymore; it was about coming out of it as something greater than themselves.

As the night grew deeper, the fire burned low, but Nathan could feel the shift in the air, a quiet determination, a collective understanding that they were all in this together.

It wasn't just the physical toll they had to endure; it was the mental game. But with each passing day, they were growing stronger, not just as soldiers, but as a unit.

"Alright, get some rest," Nathan said, standing up. "Tomorrow's going to be another long day. We push harder, we train smarter, and we do it together. Understand?"

"Yes, Sergeant!" the recruits replied in unison.

Nathan turned toward the darkness of the night, his thoughts drifting briefly to what lay ahead. It was going to get harder, he knew that. But there was something about this group. He could see it in their eyes, the spark that told him they were ready for whatever came next.

And that, he thought, was something worth fighting for.

The days blurred together, each one a gruelling test of endurance and willpower. The recruits pushed themselves through physical training, field exercises, and simulated combat scenarios. There were moments of doubt, when the weight of their gear felt unbearable, when their muscles screamed for rest, when the sun seemed relentless in its heat, but they didn't give up. They didn't falter.

Nathan kept a close eye on them, guiding them through the rough patches, offering a word of encouragement when they needed it most. He could see the change in their demeanour; the self doubt that had plagued them in the beginning had started to fade. Instead of complaining, they focused on the task at hand. They began to work with a unity that only came with shared hardship, understanding that they were all in this together.

James was no longer the hesitant, homesick recruit. His movements had become more confident, more purposeful. His face had lost some of its youthful uncertainty, replaced with a newfound focus.

He was still lanky, still not as fast as some of the others, but there was a resolve in his eyes now, a determination to push past his limits, to keep up, to prove to himself that he belonged.

Marco, on the other hand, had settled into his role as the steady anchor of the group. He may not have been the fastest or the strongest, but his experience was invaluable. He taught the younger recruits how to pace themselves, how to conserve energy for the long haul. Nathan had noticed that Marco's movements had become more deliberate as the weeks went on, his steps slower but more calculated. There was wisdom to his approach, a knowing that came from years of harder red experience.

Lieutenant Callahan continued to lead by example, always at the front during drills, pushing herself harder than anyone else. There were moments when Nathan saw her pull back, her face tight with fatigue, but she never showed weakness in front of the recruits.

She was a constant, an unmovable force of discipline and resolve.

But Nathan could see that it was beginning to take a toll on her. Her posture had started to sag ever so slightly, her movements a touch more sluggish. He'd caught her rubbing her neck after particularly intense training sessions, a small sign of the strain she was carrying. He knew she was pushing herself just as hard as the recruits, but it was starting to show.

One evening, after a particularly brutal field exercise, Nathan found her sitting alone by the fire, her eyes staring out into the darkness.

"You alright, Lieutenant?" Nathan asked as he approached, his voice softer than usual.

Callahan didn't immediately respond. She kept her gaze fixed on the flames, the crackling of the fire the only sound between them for a moment.

Finally, she turned her head slightly, just enough for Nathan to see the weariness in her eyes."I'm fine," she replied, though her voice lacked its usual conviction.

Nathan sat down beside her, offering a quiet presence. "You've been pushing yourself pretty hard. Maybe you should take a step back for a bit. Let someone else take the lead."

She shook her head, her short hair barely moving. "I can't afford to take a break. Not now. Not when they're looking to me for guidance."

"They've got you, Lieutenant," Nathan said, his tone gentle but firm. "And you've got them. It's a two way street. You can't be there for them if you're burning out yourself."

Callahan looked at him then, her eyes searching his face as if weighing his words. After a moment, she gave a small nod. "I know. But it's hard. I can't stop. Not now."

Nathan understood that. She wasn't just a leader; she was a soldier, and soldiers didn't quit. But he also knew that even the strongest of them needed to rest, to recharge.

He didn't press her any further, but he made a silent promise to himself that he'd keep an eye on her.

They couldn't afford to lose anyone, not now.

The weeks rolled on, and the training grew more intense. But with each challenge, the recruits grew stronger, more capable. They learned to anticipate each other's moves, to cover each other's backs, to work as one cohesive unit. The drills became second nature, the strategies engrained in their minds. They were no longer a group of individuals; they were a team, a family.

One afternoon, after a particularly challenging series of drills, Nathan gathered them once again around the fire. It has become a ritual now, these nightly fireside talks. The recruits were tired, their faces dirts treated and sunburned, but there was a look in their eyes that told Nathan they were ready.

"You've all come a long way," he began, his voice steady and commanding. "I've seen each of you push past limits you didn't even know you had. You've learned to trust each other, and that's the most important thing. Trust. It's what will get you through the toughest of times."

He paused, letting his words sink in. "Tomorrow, we'll face something new. It won't be easy. It might be harder than anything we've done yet.

But I want you all to remember this: no matter what happens, you've got each other.

That's your strength. And if you remember that, you'll get through anything."

The recruits sat in silence for a moment, each one digesting the weight of Nathan's words. Finally, James spoke up, his voice calm but steady.

"We'll stick together, Sergeant. We've got this."

Nathan smiled. "That's what I like to hear. Now, get some sleep. Tomorrow's going to be a long day."

As the recruits made their way to their tents, Nathan remained by the fire for a while longer, watching the flames flicker in the dark. The road ahead was still uncertain, but he knew one thing for sure: they were ready.

They had come this far, and there was no turning back now.

And, for the first time in a long time, Nathan felt a sense of pride swell within him. These recruits, his team, were no longer just a group of strangers. They were family. And together, they could face whatever came next.

The next morning came quickly, the sun barely cresting over the horizon, casting long shadows across the camp.

The air was crisp, a bite to it that sharpened the senses and woke everyone from their fitful sleep. Today's focus was weapons training, something that would push the recruits even further, testing their coordination, precision, and, most importantly, their ability to stay calm under pressure.

The recruits gathered in a large training area, a wide stretch of dirt and gravel that had been set up with various stations for different types of weapons. A series of targets, human silhouettes, lined one side, while benches, barricades, and cover points were placed strategically throughout the area.

Nathan stood in front of them, his eyes scanning the group.

"Today's the day we work on your accuracy and speed," Nathan said, his voice carrying across the still morning air. "We'll be working with everything from rifles to handguns, and a few other surprises along the way. But above all, I want you to remember one thing: calm under pressure."

He paused for a moment, letting the weight of his words sink in. "The battlefield doesn't wait for you to get your head together. You either make the shot or you don't. You either stay focused, or you get yourself, and your team, killed."

There were a few nervous glances exchanged, but Nathan could see the determination in their eyes. They were ready.

First Station Rifles.

The recruits were split into smaller groups and led to the first station, rifle training. Nathan made sure each of them was familiar with their weapon before they started.

He took James aside to give him a quick refresher.

"Focus on your stance, James," Nathan said, his hand on the young man's shoulder.

"Keep your shoulders back, elbows tucked in. You're not going for speed, not yet. You're going for accuracy. Get the feel for the weapon first."

James nodded, adjusting his grip on the rifle. He was still a bit awkward with it, but Nathan could see that he was improving. His hands were more steady than they had been weeks ago, his posture more confident. He exhaled slowly, focusing on the target downrange.

"Breathe, kid," Nathan called out. "Inhale, exhale, steady your aim. When you're ready, take the shot."

James did just that. The shot rang out, hitting the target's centre mass. It wasn't perfect, but it was close. Nathan gave him an approving nod.

"Not bad. But remember, the best shooters don't rush. Don't let the pressure of time mess with your head."

The other recruits took their turns, firing rounds in quick succession. The sounds of gunfire echoed across the range, but Nathan kept his focus on the little details, the small things that made all the difference. He watched each recruit carefully, offering feedback on their stance, their breathing, their follow through.

Second Station: Handguns

After rifle training, the recruits moved to the handgun station. The transition was jarring for some, as they were used to the longer, more stable feel of a rifle.

But Nathan knew that this was just as important, handguns were close quarters weapons, used when there was no time to reload or adjust.

Marco, despite his age and experience, seemed more comfortable with the handgun. He moved through the drills with ease, his movements steady and controlled. Nathan approached him after a round of fire, watching as Marco holstered his weapon with careful precision.

"You've got a good rhythm, Marco. What's your secret?" Nathan asked, genuinely curious.

Marco gave a small smile, his eyes crinkling at the corners. "It's all about muscle memory. You don't think, you just do. In a real fight, you don't have time to hesitate."

Nathan nodded in understanding. "You're right. That's the key. No hesitation. Just action."

As the recruits took their turns, Nathan reminded them over and over to keep their sights aligned, to avoid pulling the trigger too quickly. They needed to learn the difference between panic and precision. The handgun was a weapon that required control, especially when the distance between them and the target was close.

James struggled here more than he had with the rifle, his hands shaking slightly as he aimed. Nathan stood by, watching him carefully, then offered a quiet word of advice.

"Slow down, James," he said, his tone calm but firm. "You're not in a rush.

Focus on the fundamentals. Steady your grip, breathe, and don't let the adrenaline take over."

James nodded, resetting his stance. When he fired again, the shot was still off centre, but it was closer. He let out a small sigh of relief. It wasn't perfect, but it was progress.

Third Station: Close Combat

The next station was close combat training. This was less about the weapons and more about the mindset. The recruits had to practice with knives and their bare hands, working in pairs. They learned the basic techniques: how to disarm an opponent, how to use their body weight to control a fight, how to be quick without losing control.

Callahan stepped in here, demonstrating a disarm technique that was so fast it almost seemed like magic.

She moved with a fluidity that was mesmerising, using the attacker's own force against them.

"Remember, it's not about strength," she explained to the group. "It's about leverage, control. You need to think three moves ahead. Be ready for anything."

Nathan watched as the recruits took turns practicing the disarm drills. It was messy at first, but they were learning. They were adapting.

After hours of weapons training, the final station was a stress test. The recruits had to go through a simulated combat scenario, navigating through obstacles while being fired at from multiple angles.

They had to react to sudden changes, make quick decisions, and take the shot when it counted. The stress was designed to make them think on their feet.

Nathan watched as James and the others moved through the course. They ran, ducked behind cover, fired their weapons with precision. The air was thick with tension, the sounds of gunfire and shouted commands creating a whirlwind of noise.

James hesitated at one point, unsure of the angle, but Nathan saw the moment of clarity in his eyes.

The young recruit found his shot, steadying himself despite the surrounding chaos. When he fired, the round hit the target's dead centre.

Nathan felt a surge of pride. The recruits were starting to click, to trust their instincts. They weren't perfect, but they were getting there. They were becoming soldiers.

After Action Review

As the sun dipped below the horizon, casting a soft orange glow over the camp, Nathan gathered the recruits around for the final after action review.

"You did well today," Nathan began, his voice low and serious. "We pushed you harder than you've ever been pushed. And you responded. That's what this is all about. Not just hitting the target, but making decisions under pressure. You've learned to keep your head in the game, and that's what will keep you alive when it matters."

He glanced around at each of them, making eye contact. "But don't get cocky. This is only the beginning. You've still got a long way to go."

James, Marco, Callahan, and the others nodded, the exhaustion evident on their faces, but there was something else, too. Determination. Confidence. They were no longer just a collection of individuals. They were a team, and they had each other's backs.

Nathan gave a final nod of approval. "Alright. Get some rest. Tomorrow, we will do it all again."

As the recruits filed back to their tents, Nathan lingered for a moment, watching them. They weren't perfect, but they were improving with every passing day. And that was all he could ask for.

The days bled together, each one more demanding than the last. As the weeks passed, the intensity of the training never waned. Each day was a relentless test of endurance, skill, and mental fortitude. The recruits had gone from struggling through the basic drills to now facing scenarios that simulated real combat situations, nothing was left to chance.

Today's training would focus on an aspect Nathan had been looking forward to: tactical movement under fire. It was a test of how well the recruits could react to a fast changing battlefield while staying in formation and supporting each other. It was no longer about individual performance; it was about how well they worked together as a unit.

Nathan gathered them early in the morning, the camp still blanketed in mist. The air was thick with anticipation, the cold making their breath visible in the morning light.

"Listen up!" Nathan's voice was sharp as it cut through the air. The recruits quickly fell into formation. "Today, we're going to test your tactical movements.

This is where it gets real. We'll be running through a series of manoeuvres, and I want to see how you handle yourself under pressure. The key here is coordination. You stay together, you communicate, and you move like one unit. Got it?"

"Got it, Sergeant!" they responded in unison.

"Good. Now get your gear and follow me."

They moved quickly to the training ground. The first part of the exercise was a simple but demanding tactical drill: moving from cover to cover while under simulated fire. It wasn't just about speed, it was about staying in formation, keeping their heads down, and covering each other's movements. The recruits had to think ahead, anticipate what the others needed, and make sure they weren't leaving anyone exposed.

The drill started slowly. Nathan had them practice moving between two large walls, using hand signals to communicate with each other. Each recruit would move from one piece of cover to the next while the others provided covering fire.

They couldn't afford to get complacent; they had to anticipate the enemy's line of sight, find the best approach, and remain focused on the bigger picture.

James was up first. He looked a little nervous, but Nathan could see how far he'd come. The lanky recruit was more agile than ever, though his movements still had a sense of hesitation.

He crouched low, his rifle held tight to his chest, eyes scanning for threats.

"Move!" Nathan shouted from behind cover, signalling James to make the first move.

James bolted, staying low, moving from the first wall to the next. A few simulated gunshots rang out from the distance, meant to simulate incoming fire, but James didn't flinch. He dove into the next piece of cover, breathing hard. His focus was razor-sharp.

"Good. Stay with it," Nathan said, nodding in approval.

The others followed suit, each one taking turns to move from one piece of cover to the next. Some were quicker than others, but each of them improved with every attempt. Marco, slow but steady, moved with precision. His experience showed he always knew the best time to move, never rushing but always deliberate.

Callahan was an example of perfect coordination. Every movement was seamless. Her rifle never wavered, and her gaze was always ahead, anticipating the next move.

She was the epitome of calm under pressure. Nathan made a mental note to keep an eye on her, as she was quickly becoming a leader in her own right.

After each round of movement, Nathan gathered them together to debrief.

"You're getting better," Nathan said, his tone serious. "But don't get comfortable. The enemy won't give you time to think. They'll be just as quick, just as determined. And that means you've got to be faster and more precise. It's about instinct. You need to move before you even think about it."

They nodded, understanding the weight of his words. No one spoke; the focus in their eyes told Nathan everything he needed to know. They were ready to take it to the next level.

The second drill was the next step up, a live fire exercise, with the recruits moving through a series of obstacles while engaging targets. This would test their ability to engage threats while under the pressure of both physical exhaustion and live fire.

Nathan watched carefully, his eyes following each recruit's movements. He could see how much they had grown. They weren't just responding to commands anymore; they were anticipating what came next. They were reading to each other, working as a unit.

When it was James' turn again, he saw a noticeable improvement. His earlier hesitations had melted away, replaced by a calm resolve. He took his position behind cover and popped out just long enough to fire a quick shot at a target. He moved again, firing on the move, engaging another target in a fluid motion. His accuracy wasn't perfect, but it was much better than the first time.

"Nice job, kid," Nathan called out as James slid back into cover.

Marco wasn't as fast, but his shots were always spot on. He had a precision that came with years of experience. He knew the value of controlled movements and steady aim, and it showed. When Marco engaged his targets, it wasn't a blur of motion it was deliberate well thought out and calculated.

Callahan's movements were fluid, almost graceful. She was a natural with a rifle, her shots always landing where they needed to. But Nathan could tell she was pushing herself harder than she let on. He'd seen her rub her shoulder earlier, a subtle sign that the constant strain was wearing on her.

After the exercise, Nathan made sure to check in with each of them.

"How do you feel?" Nathan asked Marco, who was taking slow, measured breaths.

"I'm fine," Marco replied, though there was a slight edge to his voice, a sign that he was feeling the physical strain. But he wasn't about to admit it. "Just needed a second to catch my breath."

Nathan gave him a nod, understanding the unspoken truth. Marco was pushing himself to the limit, and Nathan appreciated that.

Third Drill: Team Coordination Under Stress

The final drill of the day was designed to push them to their breaking point.

It was a full team exercise where the recruits would have to clear a building, moving through tight spaces and clearing rooms while under constant fire. It was chaotic, loud, and disorienting, everything that combat could be.

The recruits moved together, clearing the building room by room, engaging targets as they went. They communicated in short, sharp bursts, always watching each other's backs. Nathan was impressed, there was no panic, no confusion.

Each recruit had their own role, and they executed it well.

James had truly stepped up. He had found his rhythm, not just in firing his weapon but in working with the team. He was watching the others' movements, anticipating the next move, covering them as they cleared rooms. It wasn't just about his own success anymore; it was about supporting the others. Nathan couldn't have been prouder.

Callahan, though clearly exhausted, was still sharp.

She was everywhere at once, leading the charge and ensuring that no one was left behind. She knew when to push forward and when to hang back. Her eyes never left the doorways, always anticipating the next threat.

Marco's deliberate movements were a stabilising force in the chaos. His methodical approach gave the group a steady foundation to build on, especially when things got tight.

At the end of the exercise, Nathan called them together for the final debriefing.

"You did well," Nathan said, his voice carrying the weight of pride.

"You've learned to move as one, to communicate without hesitation. And that's the most important thing. But we're not done yet. There's still more to learn, more to perfect."

He looked at each of them, his gaze lingering just a little longer on Callahan and Marco. "We've pushed you hard, but that's because you're capable of more. Keep this in mind: you're stronger than you think. And we're just getting started."

The recruits stood taller now, their exhaustion clear, but the fire in their eyes told Nathan everything he needed to know, they were ready for whatever came next. And, for the first time, Nathan truly believed it.

CHAPTER 3 INTO THE FIRE

Training was no longer just about physical endurance. Now, they were being tested in tactics, small unit leadership, and decision making under pressure. The intensity was unrelenting.

One morning, after weeks of nonstop drills, the recruits were assembled for a special briefing.

"Listen up!" Sergeant Walker barked. "You've all been preparing for this moment. Today, you're going to face your first real test. We're simulating an assault mission. You'll be split into teams. You'll need to work together, make decisions on the fly, and follow orders. This is what you're here for."

James's palms were sweating as he looked around. He'd never been in a real combat scenario before, and he couldn't shake the fear bubbling in his chest.

The prospect of being thrust into a high pressure environment made his heart race faster and faster.

But something in the deep pit of his stomach told him that this was exactly what he needed to become the soldier he'd always dreamed of being.

Nathan had been in similar situations many times before, but he still felt the familiar rush of adrenaline pumping around his body. Which prevented him from feeling scared, especially in front of the others.

He knew that it was important to keep his head clear, to stay focused, and to trust the people around him. This was what he had trained for, and he wasn't going to let anyone down.

The simulation was chaotic, just as war often was. Explosions rang out in the distance, and gunfire echoed through the air. The recruits sprinted, ducking behind cover, working as quickly as they could to accomplish their mission objectives. James felt his legs pumping beneath him as they stormed a mock building.

He ducked into the doorway, weapon raised, but his heart was pounding so loudly in his ears that he almost couldn't hear his teammates' commands.

"Monroe! You with us?" Marco's voice broke through the noise.

"Yeah, yeah!" James shouted, forcing himself to calm down. He squared his shoulders, forcing himself to focus on the task. He cleared a corner and moved into the next room, instinctively trusting his training.

The battle raged on, with recruits engaging in tactical manoeuvres, providing cover fire, and coordinating with each other under the watchful eyes of their instructors.

It wasn't perfect, but it was a start. By the end of the simulation, the recruits were winded but proud of what they'd accomplished.

As the last shots echoed through the training area, the recruits regrouped in the clearing outside the mock building, their bodies drenched in sweat and their minds racing from the intensity of the simulation.

Their weapons were lowered, but their eyes were sharp, each of them processing the experience in their own way.

Sergeant Walker was waiting for them, his stern face betraying no emotion.

He watched them as they gathered, then spoke with his usual authority.

"Alright, everyone, gather," he commanded. "I know that wasn't easy. This was your first real test under fire. You didn't just survive it; you got through it as a team. But don't get comfortable. This was just the beginning."

The recruits formed a semicircle around him, their tired faces betraying the exhaustion that had settled into their bones.

"James!" Walker's voice cut through the haze of fatigue. "You almost froze up back there. What happened?"

James felt the blood rush to his face. His palms were still clammy, the fear still hanging in the air around him, even though the simulation was over.

"I, uh… I was just overwhelmed, sir. I couldn't think straight. But I pushed through it," James said, his voice more steady than he felt.

Walker eyed him for a moment, as if weighing his words. "You did push through it. But listen, Monroe, that fear? It's normal. The problem is when you let it control you.

You can't afford that in the field. Next time, you need to focus on breathing, stay in the moment, and trust your training. Got it?"

"Yes, sir," James said, his voice a little stronger.

"Good. But remember, it's not just about you. It's about the team," Walker added, his gaze sweeping over the rest of the recruits. "Marco, you led your team through that breach like a pro. Your experience showed. Keep doing what you're doing."

Marco nodded, though he didn't look particularly satisfied. He was always humble, even when praise came his way.

"Callahan, you were quick to adapt, but you need to start thinking about the bigger picture.

You're a leader in the making, but you need to take more charge. I want to see you step up next time."

Callahan's sharp eyes met Walker's for a moment, acknowledging the challenge. She wasn't one to back down, and Nathan knew she would take those words to heart.

"And Nathan," Walker continued, finally turning his attention to him.

"You were steady. You kept your head in the game. But don't think that means you're untouchable. I've seen soldiers like you get complacent. You're only as good as your next decision. Never forget that."

Nathan met his gaze and gave a slight nod. He understood the weight of Walker's words. There was always room for improvement, even when it felt like you had it all figured out.

Walker gave a quick, sharp clap of his hands to get their attention once again.

"Today was a good start. But you've got a long road ahead of you.

Tomorrow, we'll run through a full after action review, and we'll see where we can improve. Rest up. You're going to need it."

With that, the recruits were dismissed, but Nathan could see the look in their eyes, they were hungry for more. They'd just faced their first real taste of battle, and while it wasn't perfect, they had survived it. And that was something.

As they made their way back to camp, Nathan fell into step beside James, who was walking a little slower, his expression lost in thought.

"How're you holding up?" Nathan asked, glancing at the young recruit.

James shot him a tight smile. "I'm fine. Just… a lot to process. I didn't think I'd get that rattled, but I did. Still, I did it. We did it."

"You did," Nathan agreed. "You pushed through when it counted. That's what matters. And you'll only get better from here."

They walked in silence for a moment before James spoke again, his voice quieter now.

"Do you ever get scared?" he asked, glancing sideways at Nathan.

Nathan was taken aback for a moment. It was a good question. It wasn't something soldiers often admitted, but it was a question he knew he had to answer honestly.

"Yeah," Nathan said, his voice low. "I do. Fear's a part of it. The trick is not letting it control you. Everyone gets scared, James.

The difference between a soldier and someone who doesn't make it is how you handle that fear. You use it to stay sharp, to keep your head in the game. It doesn't go away, but you learn how to push through it."

James nodded slowly, his face set in determination. "I think I get it now. I just have to keep going, even when it's tough."

"You're already doing that," Nathan said, giving him a reassuring slap on the back. "Just keep moving forward. That's all any of us can do."

They reached the camp, the sounds of the other recruits settling in for the night filling the air. As Nathan walked toward his tent, he couldn't help but feel a surge of pride. The recruits were making progress, and James, despite his nerves, was beginning to find his place.

The next day would bring new challenges, but Nathan knew they were ready. They had come a long way since the first day of training, and there was still so much more to teach, so much more to learn.

But as the firelight flickered in the distance and the night settled in, Nathan allowed himself a moment of quiet reflection. They were no longer just soldiers in training.

They were a team, each of them pushing themselves and each other to be better. And that was something he could be proud of.

The next morning came faster than anyone expected, and the recruits had barely slept a few hours before they were summoned for their next round of training.

The night had been restless for many of them, including James, who had spent hours tossing and turning, replaying the simulation in his head. Every corner he cleared, every burst of gunfire, every time he had nearly frozen up, it all looped over and over in his mind. But now, there was no time for second guessing.

Today, they were going deeper.

The recruits gathered once again in formation, their faces a mixture of exhaustion and determination. Sergeant Walker stood in front of them, his face set in a grim expression.

"We're not letting up," Walker said, his voice cutting through the chilly morning air.

"Today, we run the After Action Review from yesterday's mission. This isn't just about what you did right, it's about understanding what you did wrong and fixing it. Every mistake is a chance to get better. And trust me, you will make mistakes. The key is learning from them."

Nathan glanced over at James, who was standing next to him, his face set in concentration. He could see the mental gears turning in James' head. He was working through it, processing everything that had happened the day before. He could see the determination there, that spark of desire to improve.

Walker didn't waste time. He split the recruits into small groups and assigned each of them a task from the simulation to analyse. The goal wasn't just to talk about what went wrong, but to dive deeper into tactical decision making. What could they have done differently?

Where had they missed an opportunity? What was the tipping point for success or failure?

Nathan's group focused on their breach and entry into the mock building. As they debriefed, Nathan could see the others beginning to open up, each one offering their perspective on the mission.

Callahan was quick to speak up, noting how their communication had faltered during the breach.

She had been in the lead and had seen the hesitation from the others as they moved into the first room.

"We didn't communicate enough," Callahan said. "We should have called out our moves, given each other more feedback. When we rushed in, it was like we were all on our own. If we had done it slower, taken our time to reassess after each room, we could have been more efficient."

Nathan nodded. "That's a valid point. We can't rush these things. It's about control, not speed."

Marco chimed in next, his voice steady as usual. "I think we lost our focus after the first room. We cleared it, but then we didn't reassess before moving forward. It's easy to get tunnel vision in situations like that.

You clear one area, and you're focused on the next, but you forget to account for what could still be a threat behind you."

"Exactly," Nathan replied. "You've got to anticipate. Always look at the bigger picture, not just the immediate task."

James was quiet, his brow furrowed as he absorbed the conversation around him. When Nathan glanced over at him, he saw the gears turning in James' head, trying to make sense of everything.

"You good, James?" Nathan asked softly.

James looked up, a little startled, then nodded. "Yeah. Just thinking about the breach. I froze for a second. I knew we were supposed to clear fast, but I couldn't get my brain to work right. Everything was so loud, and I couldn't… I couldn't focus."

Nathan studied him for a moment, his voice firm but encouraging.

"James, that's normal. Your body is reacting to the stress of the environment. That's what you've got to train your mind to handle. It's not about being perfect, it's about pushing through that moment of hesitation. You did it, though. You came through it.

You just have to get used to that feeling, learn how to shake it off faster."

James met his eyes, his expression slightly more confident now. "I'll work on it, Sergeant. I won't let it happen again."

Nathan smiled. "That's all I need to hear. You'll get there. We all will."

The After Action Review continued with more analysis of what they could have done better. Each recruit contributed, each one examining their own role in the mission.

By the end, they had a clearer picture of how to improve. It wasn't about feeling bad for mistakes, it was about taking accountability and moving forward stronger.

When the session concluded, Walker gave them a brief moment of rest before the next exercise was announced.

"Now that we've processed what happened, it's time to test what you've learned. Today's exercise will focus on stress management and decision making under pressure. We're going to throw you into situations that will challenge your ability to think clearly when everything is going wrong.

You'll be forced to adapt, make snap decisions, and lead your team through the chaos."

James' expression shifted, and Nathan could see the unease in his eyes. But he also saw something else, determination. He wasn't going to let the pressure break him.

The training ground was set up to replicate a battlefield. It was a controlled chaos: smoke grenades went off, loud explosions simulated incoming fire, and their instructors barked commands, throwing them into scenarios that tested their reactions.

Some recruits were tasked with leading while others followed. The goal wasn't just about physical endurance, but about how well they could maintain their composure and think critically.

Nathan found himself in the thick of it almost immediately. The first scenario was a hostage rescue operation.

They had to infiltrate a building, neutralise hostile forces, and extract the hostage, all while under a heavy barrage of simulated gunfire and explosions.

It was chaos, but it was controlled chaos, and Nathan could see how everyone was stepping up in their own ways.

Callahan immediately took charge when the team was split, shouting orders and coordinating their movements with precision. Marco stayed calm under fire, picking off hostile targets with calculated shots, never rushing, always deliberate. James, though still green, had improved significantly.

He was no longer freezing up at the sound of gunfire. Instead, he moved with purpose, covering his teammates' movements, and even stepping up when the squad was pinned down, providing cover fire as the others made their way into position.

At one point, Nathan had to make a snap decision when a piece of cover they were moving toward was compromised.

He saw the danger, saw the angle of the attack, and immediately ordered his team to change direction. They moved with precision, executing the new plan without hesitation.

It was only after the scenario ended, when they were all huddled together for the debriefing, that Nathan allowed himself to relax. He could feel the weight of the training, the mental fatigue, the exhaustion, but also the pride.

They were improving. They were starting to act like a unit, not just individuals thrown together.

As Sergeant Walker came forward to lead the debrief, he nodded toward Nathan and the rest of the group.

"You all performed better than I expected. A lot of you had moments of hesitation, but you pulled through. That's what counts. The enemy isn't going to wait for you to make up your mind.

The more you do this, the faster you'll think, and the more confident you'll be in your decisions."

Nathan stood back, his arms crossed, watching his recruits.

James, Callahan, and Marco were all showing significant growth. They were learning how to think, how to lead, and how to function as a team under pressure.

It wasn't perfect, but it was progress. And that, in the end, was all Nathan could ask for.

The days that followed only got tougher. The simulation scenarios became more complex, and the recruits were pushed further beyond their limits. No longer just focused on physical endurance, the drills now tested their ability to think, to lead, to stay calm when everything was falling apart around them.

Nathan noticed a significant shift in the group. The recruits were starting to gel, to communicate more efficiently, to anticipate each other's moves. They were no longer just responding, they were planning, adapting, and making decisions before things went wrong. It was a slow but steady transformation from individuals into a cohesive unit.

James was perhaps the most visible example of this change. The young recruit who had once hesitated and faltered was now standing taller, his movements more deliberate.

His fear, though still present, had lessened. He was no longer freezing at the sound of gunfire.

Instead, he was reacting quickly, thinking on his feet. He wasn't perfect, but he was getting better.

One evening, as the group gathered around a campfire, Nathan watched James from across the fire. The young

recruit was sitting with Callahan and Marco, looking more engaged than ever before.

They were discussing the day's exercises, how to better move through urban environments, how to clear rooms more efficiently. James was talking now, offering suggestions, asking questions, taking mental notes.

Nathan had to admit, he was proud of the kid. It wasn't just about physical strength, it was about mental toughness, and James was starting to develop both.

Sergeant Walker had given them a brief break, but it wasn't going to last long.

The next morning, they were going to tackle one of their hardest challenges yet: a full day endurance test that would push them to their physical and mental limits. The recruits had no idea what to expect, but Nathan knew it wasn't going to be easy.

As they settled in for the night, Nathan pulled out a worn, tattered notebook from his pack.

It had been his training journal, kept for years, ever since he first joined the service. He had always written down lessons, observations, and thoughts after each day of training.

It had helped him process the stress, the challenges, and the lessons learned along the way.

He flipped it open to a blank page and scribbled a few quick notes. Team cohesion. Communication under pressure. Learning from mistakes.

His pen paused as his thoughts drifted to his recruits. They were still raw, still unrefined, but there was potential. It wasn't just about making it through the training, it was about learning to face fear, adversity, and hardship head on.

About becoming something bigger than themselves, something that could stand strong when the world was crumbling around them.

As he finished writing, Marco, who had been sitting quietly nearby, wandered over to him, a thoughtful look on his face.

"Everything okay, Sarge?" Marco asked, his voice low but steady.

Nathan closed the notebook and looked up. "Yeah. Just… thinking. About them. About all of you."

Marco smiled, though it didn't quite reach his eyes. "It's a tough road. But I see it too. They're starting to figure it out. Especially Monroe. Kid's got heart."

"He does," Nathan agreed. "He's come a long way. But we've got to keep pushing him. Keep pushing all of them."

Marco nodded, his eyes scanning the others, who were settling into their sleeping bags, talking quietly among themselves. "You think they're ready for what's coming?"

"I don't know," Nathan said honestly. "But we'll find out tomorrow."

The night passed quietly, but as the first light of dawn broke, the recruits were already awake, preparing for the brutal day ahead. They lined up in formation, their faces grim but determined.

The air was thick with anticipation, each of them knowing that the challenge awaiting them was going to be more demanding than anything they had faced so far.

Sergeant Walker's voice cut through the silence. "Today, you'll be tested, not just on your strength or your tactics, but on your will. You'll be pushed to the brink. Some of you will want to quit. Some of you will falter. But remember this: no matter what happens, you have a team. You will get through it together."

Nathan stood at the back, watching as Walker outlined the day's challenge. The recruits were divided into teams once again.

This time, however, the course would be a gruelling obstacle course that simulated extreme conditions, navigating through dense terrain, carrying wounded comrades, moving under simulated enemy fire, and performing complex tasks with no rest.

And just when they thought they were finished, they would have to face a final endurance test, a night navigation exercise, all while exhausted and mentally drained.

It was designed to break them.

The first few hours were punishing. The recruits moved through thick underbrush, crawled under barbed wire, scaled walls, and waded through streams. Nathan could hear the grunts of exertion, the sound of boots hitting the ground in perfect unison.

Marco was steady, never rushing but never slowing either. He seemed to know the exact pace they needed to maintain, ensuring that the team didn't burn out too early.

Callahan led the way, keeping everyone focused, her voice sharp and clear as she barked orders and encouraged them forward.

James, despite his earlier doubts, had found a new gear. He moved with purpose, his face set, his breathing steady. He was no longer the kid who froze up at the first sign of danger. He was evolving. Nathan watched him, impressed by the way he managed to keep his cool under such physical stress.

The final leg of the challenge came just as the sun began to dip below the horizon.

The recruits were exhausted, their bodies sore and covered in dirt and sweat. But there was no time to rest.

They were split into pairs and sent off to navigate through a simulated hostile environment, all while being pushed to their mental and physical limits. Their task was simple in theory: find their way through the terrain and reach an extraction point.

In reality, it was anything but simple.

Nathan watched as James and Marco moved off together. The younger recruit was now leading, navigating with a sense of calm that Nathan hadn't expected. Marco was still in charge, but James was taking charge in his own way.

They had become a unit, each pushing the other to stay focused, to keep moving, to never quit.

By the time they reached the extraction point, all of them were physically broken. But when they finally gathered, sweaty and panting, Walker surveyed them with a look of approval in his eyes.

"You all made it," Walker said, his voice softer than it had been all day.

"Not everyone would've. You've learned something today. Not just about your bodies, but about your minds. And you've learned about your team."

James looked up at Nathan, his eyes wide in disbelief. "We did it. We actually did it."

Nathan smiled, placing a hand on his shoulder. "You did it. We all did. And that's what matters."

The recruits were tired, broken, but triumphant. They had just faced their toughest test yet, and they had passed.

Months passed, and the training evolved. The recruits were finally ready for the real mission.

They had been deployed to a conflict zone, a war torn region far from home. The reality of the situation hit them hard the moment they stepped off the plane.

The air was thick with dust, the sound of distant gunfire a constant reminder that the peace they had trained to keep was elusive. Nathan could see the nervousness in the eyes of some of his soldiers, especially James, who still looked like a deer caught in headlights.

But there was no time for hesitation. They were soldiers now, and they had a job to do.

The first days were spent familiarising themselves with the terrain and meeting the local allies. They were briefed on the political situation, the enemies they would face, and the local population's expectations of the peacekeepers.

Nathan knew the complexities of such a mission all too well; the lines between friend and foe were often blurry in these kinds of operations.

The soldiers were assigned to a forward operating base (FOB), and soon enough, they were sent on their first patrol.

The environment was unforgiving: arid, barren, and scarred by conflict. Marco, who had been to places like this before, seemed oddly calm, while the others struggled to process the intensity of the surroundings.

James's hand shook as he gripped his weapon for the first time in a real world scenario. His thoughts ran away with stark realisations, that this was it, and this was the point he had trained for so hard, but now that it was happening, nothing seemed real.

He couldn't help but think of home, especially his mother, and his friends, and the life he had left behind. A sudden realisation crept into his thoughts, would he ever see them again? Would any of them?

CHAPTER 4 THE FIRST TEST

The morning air was dry and heavy, the scent of dust and sweat lingering in every breath. James adjusted his helmet and wiped his brow, feeling the weight of his rifle in his hands.

His heart raced, but he told himself to focus, focus on the training, focus on the mission. This was real. There were no do overs.

Sergeant Walker's voice echoed over the comms as the convoy of armoured vehicles rumbled toward their first objective, a small village suspected of harbouring insurgents.

"Stay sharp," Walker said, his voice steady but laced with urgency. "This isn't a training exercise anymore. Expect resistance. We move in, clear the area, and establish a presence. Follow orders, and stay together."

James swallowed hard and glanced over at Marco, who was riding shotgun in their vehicle. Marco's face was unreadable, his eyes scanning the horizon, as if he were already mentally preparing for what was coming.

Nathan, in the vehicle behind them, caught James's gaze through the rearview mirror and gave him a small, reassuring nod.

"We're in this together," Nathan had said before they'd left base.

The convoy came to a stop as the first vehicle's engine sputtered to a halt. The rest of them followed suit, parking in a tight formation, weapons raised, eyes scanning the area. James's mouth went dry as the dust settled, the village in front of them eerily quiet. There was a stillness here that was almost suffocating.

"Move out," Walker barked.

The soldiers dismounted quickly, the sound of boots hitting the ground reverberating in the thick air. Nathan's voice came over James's headset.

"Stay close, Monroe. Don't wander. You've got this."

James nodded, even though his stomach was twisting into knots.

He'd practiced everything in boot camp, taking down targets, clearing rooms, maintaining a steady position. But nothing in training had prepared him for this.

Not the oppressive heat, not the uncertainty of whether someone was waiting just around the corner with a rifle aimed at his head.

As they moved deeper into the village, James could see the signs of conflict everywhere, burnt out vehicles, homes with broken windows, the faint sound of a woman crying from a nearby building. It was surreal.

This was no longer an exercise, no longer a drill. This was real life, and the stakes were higher than ever.

They approached a cluster of buildings that seemed to be abandoned. Walker motioned for them to spread out and sweep the area. James stuck to Nathan's side, heart pounding as they checked each room.

The buildings were mostly empty, furniture overturned, walls riddled with bullet holes. But then, as they reached the last building, a voice called out from inside.

"Please, don't shoot! We are civilians!"

James froze. His breath caught in his throat. A civilian. Could they trust this? Was it a trap?

Nathan signalled for the others to hold position as he carefully approached the door. "Stay behind me," he muttered to James.

With a quick motion, he kicked the door open, and they were met with the sight of a man, his arms raised in surrender. Behind him, a woman and child huddled in the corner.

"Are you alone?" Nathan asked, his voice firm but not unkind.

The man nodded frantically. "Yes! Yes! Please, don't hurt us."

James's mind raced. This was the kind of decision they'd been trained for, how to deal with civilians in the middle of a conflict zone. He had heard horror stories of soldiers who had made mistakes, of misjudging situations and making choices they couldn't undo.

"Are you armed?" Nathan asked, his gaze never leaving the man.

"No… no, just us," the man stammered. His hands shook.

Nathan nodded. "Alright, get down. Stay down and stay quiet. We'll clear the rest of the village. Stay inside until we leave."

The family nodded and huddled together in the corner, fear written across their faces. James took a deep breath, feeling the weight of the decision.

This was what they were here for, to protect civilians, to keep the peace. But even as he made the decision to let them go, he knew there was always the chance that someone would use this as a trap.

He couldn't shake the doubt gnawing at him. But they had no choice. The mission was clear.

They continued their sweep through the village, making sure to check every building and alleyway. It felt like an eternity, each moment dragging on with the tension of not knowing who was watching them.

But as they moved toward their extraction point, nothing else occurred. No insurgents, no traps. Just the still, unsettling quiet of a place torn apart by violence.

As the convoy left the village, James's mind raced with the images of the family they'd just encountered.

He had expected danger, he had expected to face armed resistance. But seeing the fear in those civilians' eyes made him question everything. Was this really about protecting them, or was it about something else?

Days passed, and the missions continued. The soldiers were sent on a variety of operations, patrols, searches, and, eventually, direct confrontations with insurgent forces. But every mission left James with more questions than answers.

The further they pushed into hostile territory, the harder it became to distinguish friend from foe.

Local civilians were often caught in the crossfire, sometimes even fighting alongside insurgents for their own reasons.

The lines blurred, and James began to see the complexity of the situation. It wasn't black and white. It was grey, and sometimes, that made the decisions even harder.

One day, the platoon was tasked with securing a supply route. It was a simple mission in theory: to clear the area, ensure it was safe for convoy trucks carrying food and medical supplies, but the reality was far different.

As they approached the area, the sound of gunfire erupted from a nearby hilltop. The insurgents had set up a position to ambush them.

The convoy came to a screeching halt as the first shots rang out, and the soldiers immediately dropped into cover, returning fire.

The air filled with the deafening noise of combat, and James found himself taking cover behind a low wall, his rifle aimed at the enemy position.

"Monroe, stay with me!" Nathan shouted over the noise. "You're on the left flank. Cover the entrance!"

James's hands were shaking as he moved to his position, his mind struggling to focus through the adrenaline and chaos. He could feel his heart pounding in his chest as he aimed at the insurgents, who were barely visible behind rocks and dirt mounds.

He squeezed the trigger, sending rounds toward the enemy, but it felt like he was detached from reality, like he was watching it happen rather than being part of it.

"Move! Move! We need to push forward!"
Walker ordered.

They charged, pushing up the hill with rifle fire
sparking around them. The insurgents didn't give
up easily, and the firefight raged on. James's
breath came in ragged gasps as they closed the
distance. Finally, the enemy position was
overwhelmed, but not without casualties.

One of the soldiers in their unit, Private Harris,
had been hit. The medic rushed to him, but it
was too late, Harris had already been struck in
the chest. His eyes were wide with shock, and his
breathing was shallow.

Nathan's face tightened as he ordered the squad
to fall back. "Get him to the chopper," he
barked, his voice taut with anger. "We're not
leaving anyone behind."

But as the soldiers carried Harris away, James
couldn't shake the image of the young man's
lifeless eyes. He had just been talking to him that
morning, sharing a laugh over the mess hall
breakfast. Now, he was gone.

War wasn't just about the enemies you fought, it
was about the cost you paid. The price of each
decision, of each bullet fired. It was about
sacrifice.

And James was beginning to realise that the true toll of war wasn't just the physical wounds, it was the emotional scars that no one could see.

The convoy moved on after the firefight, but the weight of what had just happened hung in the air like a dark cloud. The sound of the engine's hum was a distant thrum in James's ears as he sat, staring out the window of the armoured vehicle.

He kept replaying Harris's final moments in his mind. Gone. Just like that. A young life extinguished in an instant, with no time to say goodbye, no time to process it.

Nathan was beside him in the vehicle, watching the road ahead with a sharp, practiced eye. His jaw was tight, his expression unreadable.

The loss of one of their own always hit hard, especially when it was someone like Harris, someone so full of life, someone who had a laugh that could fill the whole room.

Nathan's silence spoke volumes. He had been in this situation before, and each time, it cut deeper.

They had been close to securing the supply route, but now there was a heavy sense of emptiness hanging over the platoon. The objective had been achieved, but it felt hollow in the face of loss.

The sun was setting when they finally reached their new position, a secured outpost where they were to rest for the night. The atmosphere was somber.

The soldiers dismounted, mechanically going about their business, setting up camp with little conversation.

They knew what had to be done, cleaning weapons, checking equipment, making sure everything was ready for the next day.

James sat down with his rifle resting across his knees, his thoughts a whirlwind. The desert air was hot, dry against his skin. He felt the weight of the world on his shoulders, his uncertainty, his fears, and now, the burden of the lives lost, of the decisions made in the heat of combat.

"Monroe," Nathan's voice came from behind, steady but with an edge of concern. "You alright?"

James didn't turn to face him at first.

He could hear the subtle crack in Nathan's voice, the kind that only came from someone who had seen far too much.

Finally, James spoke, his voice quiet, almost hollow. "I don't know, Sarge. I… I'm just trying to make sense of all of this."

Nathan sat down beside him, his eyes scanning the camp before resting on James.

"There's no making sense of it, kid. Not in the way you want. War's messy. It doesn't fit into neat little boxes."

"You'll never have all the answers, and you'll never know if you did the right thing, even when you think you did."

James nodded slowly, trying to absorb the weight of Nathan's words. He had been taught to follow orders, to execute the mission with precision, to protect his team at all costs. But now, in the quiet aftermath, all those rules seemed to blur.

The faces of civilians, the sound of Harris's laugh before the fight, the cries of the innocent, it all tangled together, and he couldn't untangle it.

"What if I made the wrong call?" James asked, his voice barely more than a whisper.

Nathan's gaze hardened, but there was understanding in his eyes. "You don't get to second guess yourself out here. The decisions are too important, and the consequences too high. You made the call based on what you knew at the time.

 And that's all any of us can do. What matters now is that you keep moving forward. For yourself. For Harris. For all of us."

James swallowed hard, his throat tight. "I just… I don't know if I'm cut out for this, Sarge."

Nathan sighed, looking up at the fading light of the sunset. "You're cut out for it if you're willing to learn. This isn't something anyone can be born ready for.

It's something you have to earn every day. And you've come a long way, Monroe. The kid who barely kept up is not the same guy sitting next to me now."

James didn't respond, but the words settled deep in his chest. He had changed, there was no denying that.

He was no longer the wide eyed recruit he had been when he first set foot on base. He had learned hard lessons, witnessed brutality, and made decisions that would haunt him for the rest of his life. But he had also learned to lead, to trust in his brothers and sisters in arms, and to face fear head on.

Nathan's hand clapped gently on his shoulder. "You've got a long way to go, but that's the way it works. We all do."

As night fell and the camp settled into an uneasy silence, James thought about what Nathan had said. Keep moving forward. It seemed like the only thing he could do now. One step at a time.

The days that followed were a blur of missions, ambushes, and firefights. The soldiers had become accustomed to the uncertainty that defined their every movement.

They went through the motions, clearing buildings, engaging in combat, performing their duties, but the weight of what they had lost, of what they had seen, was always there, hanging like a shadow over them.

For James, the toll was beginning to show.

His eyes were always on edge, his movements more deliberate, like he was calculating the cost of each action.

There was no such thing as a simple decision anymore. Every action, every order, had consequences, some immediate, some that wouldn't reveal themselves until much later.

One evening, after a particularly rough mission, James stood at the edge of the camp, looking out at the darkening horizon. The stars were beginning to appear, faint pinpricks of light in the vast, empty sky.

For a moment, he felt small, insignificant in the face of everything that had happened, everything he had witnessed.

But then he remembered Nathan's words. Keep moving forward. He wasn't sure if he would ever find peace with what had happened, if he would ever have all the answers, but he knew that he had to keep going. He had a job to do.

He had a team to protect. And that was all that mattered now.

The days turned into weeks, and the missions continued to come one after another, each more intense than the last.

The desert landscape stretched out before them like a vast, empty expanse, a constant reminder of the distance between them and everything they had left behind.

James had grown used to the tension that hung in the air, the quiet moments between firefights when every sound seemed amplified, every shadow a potential threat. He could feel it in his bones now, the pressure of the decisions they had to make, the weight of their rifles, the quiet hum of their equipment.

The night after their most recent mission was no different. They were set up in a temporary base camp, the sounds of distant chatter and the occasional burst of laughter barely audible over the crackling fire.

Nathan had pulled him aside, giving him a moment to breathe, to talk, something that had become rare during the brutal grind of the past few weeks.

"Monroe, sit," Nathan said, gesturing to the ground beside him. "You look like you've been running on empty."

James hesitated but dropped to the ground next to Nathan, his rifle leaning against his leg. The firelight flickered across Nathan's face, making the deep lines of fatigue around his eyes more noticeable.

The man had seen more than his fair share of battles, and it was beginning to show.

"I'm fine," James replied, though it wasn't entirely true. "Just thinking about the next mission."

Nathan chuckled softly, but it wasn't a laugh of humour, it was the tired chuckle of a soldier who had learned to push through exhaustion and fear.

"You're always thinking about the next mission. That's the job, I guess.

But don't forget to check in with yourself every now and then, Monroe. You're not just a soldier. You're a person, too."

James looked down at his hands, noticing how they were still trembling slightly from the last firefight. He knew Nathan was right.

He had been so focused on the tasks at hand, on the constant need to stay alert and keep moving forward, that he hadn't stopped to think about how the war was changing him.

"It's just… it never ends," James said quietly, his voice betraying a weariness he hadn't realised he was carrying. "Every time we finish a mission, another one is right around the corner. It feels like there's no end in sight."

Nathan nodded slowly, his eyes reflecting the flickering flames. "That's because there isn't, not for us. Not for soldiers. The job isn't about finding the end. It's about how you get through each day.

Each moment. Some days are harder than others. Some days, you're just surviving. And that's okay. You've got to make peace with that."

James glanced at Nathan, sensing there was more to what he was saying. "How do you do it?" he asked quietly. "How do you keep going when it feels like you're just losing everything?"

Nathan didn't answer right away. He stared into the fire for a long moment, as if the answer was hidden somewhere within the flames.

Then, he spoke, his voice quieter than usual. "You don't keep going for yourself, kid. You do it for the guy next to you. For the team. For those who can't be here anymore. Because when you stop, when you give up, the mission dies with you. And we don't let that happen. Not on our watch."

James took a deep breath, letting the weight of those words sink in. It was true, in a way. Every decision they made, every move they took, was for others, the ones who were still alive, the ones who depended on them. He had learned to rely on his team, but he hadn't truly understood why until now.

As the night wore on, the fire burned low, casting long shadows over the camp. The sounds of distant conversation began to fade as the soldiers settled into their tents for the night. James lay back on the hard ground, staring up at the stars. They felt so far away, so distant from the chaos and violence below.

He thought about the family they had encountered in the village, how they had been so afraid, how they had pleaded for their lives.

He had been conflicted then, torn between the responsibility to protect them and the fear that he might be making a mistake. But now, with the quiet weight of Nathan's words hanging in the air, he understood. It wasn't always about the right or wrong choice at the moment.

It was about staying true to what they were here for, protecting those who couldn't protect themselves, and doing it together.

The next day, they were on the move again, heading to a new location, a new mission. James felt the familiar weight of his rifle in his hands, the responsibility of the mission ahead heavy on his shoulders.

He wasn't sure what the day would bring, but he was starting to understand that it didn't matter. It was the people around him that mattered.

"Stay sharp, Monroe," Nathan said, his voice steady as always. "We've got each other's backs. Don't forget that."

James nodded, his resolve hardening. "I won't."

The convoy rumbled to life, and as the vehicles rolled out, James glanced at his team, at Marco, who had his usual calm demeanour, at Lieutenant Callahan, who was always at the forefront, leading by example, and at Nathan, who was steady and unshaken no matter how bad things got.

He was surrounded by people he could trust.

For the first time in a while, James felt a spark of hope. They were in this together. And together, they could make it through whatever the mission threw at them.

The sun rose high in the sky as the convoy rumbled through the rugged terrain.

The air felt thick with tension, a quiet anticipation settling over the soldiers as they neared their next objective.

This mission was different. It wasn't just about clearing an area or securing a route; it was about a high value target. Intelligence had suggested that a key insurgent leader was hiding in the vicinity of a small compound, a compound that was heavily fortified.

The plan was straightforward: infiltrate, capture, and extract. No room for mistakes. The risk was high, and so was the potential reward. The insurgent leader could be the key to dismantling a major part of their operations.

But James knew better than to get too attached to the idea of success. Every mission could change in an instant.

"Alright, listen up," Sergeant Walker's voice crackled over the comms. "We're approaching the target. Keep your heads in the game. This is no longer a drill. Stay sharp. Monroe, I want you to stick with Nathan. No wandering off."

They arrived at the outskirts of the compound just before dusk, the fading light casting long shadows over the barren landscape. The team dismounted, moving quickly into position. The compound sat nestled between two low hills, the perimeter lined with razor wire and makeshift barricades. It was heavily guarded.

"We'll breach from the east," Walker said, pointing to the map he had spread out on the hood of their lead vehicle.

"Monroe, you're with Nathan and Callahan on point. Marco, you and your team will provide overwatch. If we get pinned down, we'll fall back to the extraction point."

James nodded, his pulse quickening. They'd trained for this. They knew the drill. But nothing could prepare them for the real deal. The sound of boots crunching against the gravel was the only sound as the soldiers moved into position, weapons at the ready.

The plan was simple: breach the compound, eliminate any resistance, and capture the target. James glanced at Nathan, who was checking his rifle, the calm and methodical movements putting James at ease, even if just slightly.

Nathan caught his gaze and gave him a brief nod, signalling that it was time to go.

"On me," Nathan said, his voice low but clear.

They approached the east wall of the compound, sticking to the shadows. Callahan moved up beside them, her eyes scanning for any movement. The tension in the air was thick enough to cut with a knife, and James couldn't help

but feel the weight of what was about to happen. This wasn't a training exercise. People could die.

They reached the breach point. Callahan set the charge and took a step back, signalling for everyone to get ready.

"Stand by," she said, her voice steady.

A few seconds later, the explosion rang out, sending a blast of dust and debris into the air. The wall crumbled, creating a jagged opening into the compound. Without missing a beat, the team moved on.

The compound was dimly lit, shadows dancing across the walls as they advanced. They moved quickly, clearing rooms one by one, the familiar routine of checking corners, covering each other, and listening for the slightest sound.

The air was thick with the smell of dust, sweat, and something more metallic, a smell that James had come to associate with the reality of combat.

They reached the centre of the compound, and that's when the firefight started.

Gunfire erupted from a hidden position, and the team ducked for cover. James felt the sting of adrenaline hit his bloodstream, and his senses sharpened.

He dropped to a knee, using the corner of the building as cover, and squeezed off a few rounds, hoping to suppress the enemy's fire.

"Monroe, move!" Nathan's voice came through his earpiece, pulling him from his thoughts. "We've got to push through. Move!"

James didn't hesitate. He popped out from behind cover, sprinting toward the next position. The sound of gunfire was deafening, but he kept moving, kept his eyes fixed on his target. He trusted Nathan, trusted Callahan, and most importantly, he trusted his training.

They reached the building where the insurgent leader was believed to be hiding. Nathan kicked the door open, and they flooded in. Inside, it was quiet, too quiet. James's heart raced as they moved through the dimly lit hallway, weapons raised.

"Clear!" Callahan called from the first room.

James's breath caught in his throat as they pushed forward. And then they found him.

The insurgent leader was standing in a small office at the back of the building, his hands raised in surrender.

He was older than James had imagined, with a hard look in his eyes that didn't seem to match the desperation in his voice.

"Please," the man said, his voice ragged. "I'm not the one you want. They're the ones you should be after. Please, listen…"

Nathan stepped forward, his gun still trained on the man. "Shut up," he growled. "Get on the ground, now."

The insurgent leader hesitated for just a moment before complying, dropping to his knees. The tension in the room was palpable, and James could feel the weight of the moment.

They had him. But as the man's eyes darted nervously around the room, something didn't sit right with him.

"Is he the one?" James asked, his voice tight with uncertainty.

"Doesn't matter," Nathan replied, his tone flat. "He's going to the intel team, whether he's the one or not. We've got our orders."

With the target in custody, they started the long, tense trek back to the extraction point.

The firefight had quieted down, and the convoy waited for them at the edge of the compound. The soldiers were on high alert, scanning the horizon for any signs of a counterattack.

James couldn't shake the feeling that something was wrong. There was a heaviness in the air that lingered, a gnawing sense of unease. They had completed the mission, but what did it all really mean? Would capturing this man lead to the dismantling of the insurgency? Or was it just another piece in a much larger puzzle that no one had the answers to?

As they loaded the target into the convoy, Nathan clapped him on the back.

"Good job today, Monroe," he said, his voice sincere.

James nodded, but the words felt hollow in his mouth. They had won this battle, but the war was far from over.

The convoy rumbled back toward their base, the dust swirling in their wake, as the weight of the mission settled heavily on James's shoulders.

The man they had captured was secured in the back of one of the armoured vehicles, bound and gagged, his eyes darting nervously between the soldiers around him.

The tension was palpable, and for a moment, James wondered if the insurgent leader was right, if they were chasing shadows.

Nathan's voice broke through his thoughts. "You good, Monroe?"

James nodded stiffly, his eyes locked on the horizon. "Yeah… just thinking."

"I get it," Nathan replied, his voice calm. "But right now, we don't have time for think. We've got to keep moving. Focus on what's next."

The words stung more than James expected. He didn't want to feel like this was all just a machine, running from one mission to the next with no space for the kind of reflection that kept his humanity intact. But Nathan was right.

The mission wasn't over. They had a prisoner to extract, intelligence to collect, and a thousand other questions they couldn't answer yet.

By the time they reached the base, night had fallen, and the stars were barely visible through the haze of smoke and dust. The camp was quieter now, the sounds of distant gunfire and occasional explosions becoming part of the backdrop to their daily existence.

As the convoy parked and the soldiers disembarked, the tension from the mission began to dissolve, but a strange heaviness remained in the air.

Sergeant Walker was waiting for them at the entrance to the command tent. He wasn't smiling. In fact, his face was stern as he approached Nathan and the others.

"We've got a problem," Walker said, his voice low but urgent. "Intel just came in. That man we captured? He's not the one we thought he was."

James felt a chill run down his spine. Not the one we thought he was?

"What does that mean?" Nathan asked, his expression hardening.

Walker didn't hesitate. "It means we've got bigger fish to fry. The real target is still out there, and he's one step ahead of us. We were set up. The whole mission was a diversion."

The words hit James like a punch to the gut. A diversion? Everything they had just gone through, everything they had risked, was for nothing?

"Who's the real target?" Callahan asked, her voice edged with anger.

Walker paused, glancing at the soldiers around him, then leaned in closer. "He's a ghost. We've been tracking him for months, but he's always one step ahead. Our source, the one who gave us the intel on the compound, has been feeding us lies."

James's mind raced. They had been betrayed, by someone on the inside. But the question that gnawed at him was how far this deception ran. If their source had been compromised, then who else had been playing them?

"This isn't just about insurgents anymore," Walker continued. "It's about trust. Someone in this operation is feeding them information. And I want to know who."

The weight of the words sank into the pit of James's stomach. They weren't just fighting a war; they were fighting a war of deception, one that was slowly unraveling everything they had believed in.

Nathan spoke first, his voice tight with barely contained fury. "So what's the plan now?"

Walker straightened, his gaze cold. "We're going after the real target. But this time, we do it right. No more false leads. I need every single one of you to stay sharp. No mistakes."

Chapter 5 The Burden of Loss

The rest of the night was a blur of debriefs, strategy sessions, and planning. James barely spoke as the hours passed, his thoughts consumed with the realisation that this mission had been a test, not just of their combat skills, but of their trust in one another. And now that trust has been fractured.

As dawn approached, the team gathered in the briefing room, their eyes bloodshot from lack of sleep but their resolve hardening. Sergeant Walker had laid out a new plan. They would move out in the morning, this time with a different objective.

"The target is moving," Walker said, pointing to a map of the region. "We've tracked him to a location near the border. We hit fast and hard; no hesitation."

James's stomach twisted as he looked at the map, trying to process the magnitude of what was coming next. This wasn't just about capturing an insurgent leader anymore. This was about securing the future of their operation, and potentially the lives of everyone involved.

"Monroe," Nathan's voice broke through his thoughts, "you okay?"

James glanced up, surprised by the concern in his voice. It was a rare thing for Nathan to show vulnerability, but at that moment, it was as if he could see the storm brewing inside James's head.

"I'm fine," James muttered, though it felt like a lie. He wasn't sure if he could be fine anymore.

The last few weeks had shattered his illusions of what this war was really about. And now, the lines between right and wrong are more blurred than ever before.

"You're more than fine," Nathan said with a small, knowing smile. "You've got this. We've all got this."

The words didn't quite sink in, but the reassurance in Nathan's voice helped steady James's nerves. He had to stay focused. They had to finish this, whatever it was. For the team. For their survival.

As they prepared to move out, James couldn't shake the feeling that this mission would be different. That would change everything.

And as the convoy pulled out of the base and into the early morning light, he couldn't help but wonder what kind of man he would become after it was all over.

The rest of the night was a blur of debriefs, strategy sessions, and planning. James barely spoke as the hours passed, his thoughts consumed with the realisation that this mission had been a test, not just of their combat skills, but of their trust in one another. And now that trust has been fractured.

As dawn approached, the team gathered in the briefing room, their eyes bloodshot from lack of sleep but their resolve hardening. Sergeant Walker had laid out a new plan. They would move out in the morning, this time with a different objective.

"The target is moving," Walker said, pointing to a map of the region. "We've tracked him to a location near the border. We hit fast and hard; no hesitation."

James's stomach twisted as he looked at the map, trying to process the magnitude of what was coming next. This wasn't just about capturing an insurgent leader anymore. This was about securing the future of their operation, and potentially the lives of everyone involved.

"Monroe," Nathan's voice broke through his thoughts, "you okay?"

James glanced up, surprised by the concern in his voice. It was a rare thing for Nathan to show vulnerability, but at that moment, it was as if he could see the storm brewing inside James's head.

"I'm fine," James muttered, though it felt like a lie. He wasn't sure if he could be fine anymore. The last few weeks had shattered his illusions of what this war was really about. And now, the lines between right and wrong are more blurred than ever before.

"You're more than fine," Nathan said with a small, knowing smile. "You've got this. We've all got this."

The words didn't quite sink in, but the reassurance in Nathan's voice helped steady James's nerves. He had to stay focused. They had to finish this, whatever it was. For the team. For their survival.

As they prepared to move out, James couldn't shake the feeling that this mission would be different. That would change everything.

And as the convoy pulled out of the base and into the early morning light, he couldn't help but wonder what kind of man he would become after it was all over.

The convoy sped through the arid landscape, kicking up dust in the early morning light. The tension in the air was palpable, the weight of the mission hanging over them like a storm cloud.

James sat quietly in the back of the vehicle, his fingers gripping the edge of his rifle, his mind racing through everything they had just learned. This wasn't just about taking down insurgents anymore.

It was about trust and betrayal. The lines between right and wrong had already blurred, and now, they were about to chase a ghost, a man who had outsmarted them at every turn.

James glanced over at Nathan, who sat across from him, his eyes scanning the horizon with quiet intensity. Despite the circumstances, Nathan seemed calm, almost detached, as if he had already accepted whatever came next.

James, however, couldn't shake the feeling that everything was unraveling faster than they could keep up.

"Monroe," Nathan's voice was low, steady, "I need you to focus on the mission. It's easy to get lost in the details, but right now, the only thing that matters is what's in front of us."

James nodded, swallowing hard. He appreciated Nathan's confidence, but the weight of the situation was starting to gnaw at him. They had been betrayed. And the worst part? They didn't know who to trust anymore.

The convoy made it's way closer to the border, the landscape shifting from dry plains to more rugged terrain. The further they went, the more isolated the area became.

No civilian structures, no signs of life, just vast stretches of nothingness.

The silence felt unnerving, like they were entering a place that didn't belong in the world they knew.

As they approached the target area, Sergeant Walker's voice came over the comms. "This is it. We're minutes away from the target's location.

No more mistakes, people. Stay tight and stay sharp. We're going in hot."

The convoy slowed, the vehicles moving in sync as they navigated a narrow path between jagged hills. James's heart rate spiked, his breath coming faster as the adrenaline kicked in. They were close, closer than ever before to the person who had been pulling the strings behind the scenes.

The thought that they might finally end the pursuit brought a strange mixture of relief and dread.

"We're going in silent," Walker continued, his voice now a whisper over the comms.

"We get in, we clear the area, and we secure the target. Remember, this guy has friends. Watch your six."

The convoy came to a halt. The soldiers dismounted quickly, weapons raised, moving in tight formations. James followed Nathan's lead as they moved toward a low ridge, crouching low to avoid detection.

His heart pounded in his chest as they approached the objective, the target area just over the next rise.

There was no time to think. Only time to act.

The plan was simple: get in, find the target, and neutralise the threat. But simplicity in war rarely equates to ease. As they crested the rise, James's breath caught in his throat. Ahead of them lay a fortified compound, surrounded by guards and fortified positions.

It wasn't the simple hideout they had been expecting. This was a well constructed operation, complete with watch towers, barriers, and armed sentries on every corner.

This wasn't just an insurgent base. This was a well established operation, a nest of vipers.

"Walker, we've got company," Marco's voice crackled over the comms.

"Roger that," Walker replied, his tone sharp. "We adjusted the plan. Monroe, you're with me. We're going to flank right. Nathan, Callahan, take the left. We push in fast and hard. No hesitation."

James's stomach twisted as they moved into position. The plan was clear, too clear.

They had to break in and catch the target before he could escape, but with so many guards, the odds weren't in their favour.

"Stay low. Stay quiet," Nathan muttered, his voice barely audible as they crouched behind a cluster of rocks, watching the compound through their scopes.

James could feel the tension coiling in his chest, but he forced himself to breathe. The plan was solid. They could do this. They had trained for this.

Nathan gave him a quick nod before signalling to Callahan. They began to move, a coordinated effort to strike fast and disorient the enemy. James and Walker followed, slipping through the shadows like ghosts, closing in on the compound with lethal intent.

The minutes stretched on like hours. James's muscles burned as he held his position, watching for any movement. The compound was alive with activity, but there was no sign of the target yet.

The air was thick with the scent of dirt and tension.

Suddenly, a shout rang out from one of the sentries. "Intruders!"

The moment the alarm sounded, chaos erupted. The enemy soldiers scrambled into position, guns raised. James's heart leaped into his throat as gunfire erupted around them, the crack of bullets flying past him as he dove for cover.

His training kicked in, his rifle steady as he returned fire, suppressing the enemy positions with quick, controlled bursts.

"Push forward!" Walker shouted. "Stay on him! Don't let them regroup!"

James moved with the others, the sound of his heartbeat pounding in his ears. He couldn't afford to hesitate, not now. They were in it, fully committed. And he was right there with them.

They reached the compound's edge, and Walker gave the signal to breach. The door exploded in a shower of splinters, and they stormed in, rifles raised. The building was dark, the air thick with dust.

They cleared the rooms methodically, checking corners, searching for the target. It wasn't long before they found him.

The target was holed up in the back of the compound, surrounded by a group of armed men. He wasn't the faceless enemy James had imagined. The man looked tired, haggard, but he was still dangerous.

His eyes flicked from one soldier to the next, calculating his chances.

"Don't move!" Walker barked.

But the target didn't listen. He moved quickly, reaching for a weapon, and the room erupted in a hail of gunfire. James fired first, hitting the target square in the chest. The man collapsed to the ground with a sickening thud.

The mission was over.

But as James stood there, rifle still raised, his body trembling from the rush of adrenaline, something inside him felt hollow. They had completed their objective, but at what cost? The air felt different now, more oppressive.

He glanced at Nathan, who was watching him, an expression unreadable.

"Good job, Monroe," Nathan said, his voice steady.

James nodded slowly, but the words didn't feel real. The victory felt like a weight on his chest, a reminder that in war, there were no true winners. Only those who survived.

As the team moved to extract the target's intel, James knew the battle wasn't over. Not by a long shot.

And as they made their way back to base, he couldn't help but wonder: how much more of this could he take before he lost himself in the chaos?

The cost of war was far greater than he'd ever imagined.

The ride back to base was eerily quiet. The usual chatter among the team was absent, replaced by the hum of the vehicle's engine and the occasional crackle of the radio. James sat in the back, his body stiff, his mind still reeling from the firefight.

He stared at his rifle, his hands still trembling from the adrenaline, though the fight had long since ended.

The image of the target's body, his final, desperate movement as he reached for a weapon, kept replaying in James's mind.

The moment he pulled the trigger felt like a lifetime. It wasn't the first time he had taken a life, but each time, it felt different. Each time, it felt heavier.

James shifted uncomfortably, trying to shake off the weight of it. He glanced around at the others. Nathan was sitting across from him, looking out the window, his face unreadable. Marco was next to him, his hands resting on his lap, eyes closed, but James could see the slight tension in his posture.

Callahan, who usually held a commanding presence, was silently cleaning her weapon. Everyone seemed to be lost in their own thoughts, processing the mission in their own way.

It wasn't until they hit the gates of the base that the silence broke.

"Alright, people," Sergeant Walker's voice crackled over the radio. "You've done your job. Now get your gear and get some rest. We'll debrief later."

James didn't need to be told twice. As soon as the vehicle stopped, he was out of it, his boots hitting the dirt with a solid thud. The sun was setting, casting a long shadow over the camp.

He walked in silence, his mind clouded, his emotions a mess of confusion and guilt. The weight of the kill was still fresh in his chest, and it wasn't going away anytime soon.

"Monroe!" Nathan's voice broke through his thoughts.

James stopped and turned. Nathan was standing a few feet away, watching him closely.

"You good?" Nathan asked, his expression softening slightly.

James opened his mouth to reply, but the words didn't come. He wasn't sure what to say. Was he good? How could he be? After everything that had just happened, after everything he had seen, could anyone ever be "good"?

"I'll be fine," he finally muttered, his voice rough.

Nathan didn't push it. Instead, he nodded, his eyes flicking toward the mess hall where the rest of the unit was headed.

"Come on," Nathan said, his voice low. "Let's get something to eat. You'll feel better after some chow."

James nodded again, but it wasn't the food he was hungry for. It was answers. And he knew deep down that he wasn't going to get any. At least, not yet.

The mess hall was crowded, as it always was after a mission. Soldiers milled about, talking in low voices, their faces haggard and tired from the day's events. James took a seat at one of the empty tables, picking at the bland food on his tray. He didn't have much of an appetite, but he knew he needed to eat, to fuel up for whatever came next.

Nathan sat across from him, as if he knew that James needed the company.

"You did good out there," Nathan said after a long pause, his eyes meeting James's. "I know it's hard, but you did your job. And you did it well."

James looked down at his food, trying to process Nathan's words. The praise didn't feel like much. It didn't change what had happened. It didn't erase the death. It didn't make it easier.

"I don't know if I can keep doing this," James said, his voice barely above a whisper. "I mean… I thought I could. I thought I knew what I was getting into. But this… it's not what I expected. The weight of it. The decisions. I don't know how to live with it."

Nathan was silent for a moment, as if considering his words carefully. When he spoke again, his voice was low, but firm.

"You'll learn," he said simply. "You have to. It's part of the job. No one comes out of this the same. But you're still you. Just… a different version of you. We all are. We're all carrying our own burdens. But you don't carry them alone.

We're a team. We have each other's backs. And that's what gets us through."

James wasn't sure he believed it, but he nodded anyway. The truth was, Nathan's words had always had a way of making things feel a little less impossible. But that didn't change the fact that he was still struggling with what he had become what they had all become.

After dinner, they gathered for the debrief. It was the same routine as always: sit, listen, answer questions, get assigned to the next task. But today, it felt different. The tension in the room was thick.

Everyone was on edge, knowing that this wasn't just another mission, it was the beginning of something bigger.

"Listen up," Sergeant Walker said, his voice cutting through the low murmurs of the room. "The target we took down today wasn't just any insurgent.

He's connected. We've got intel that he was part of a larger network that's been causing problems across multiple regions.

What you did today was a small piece of the puzzle. But we've got a bigger picture to deal with now.

More work, more risks. And it won't get any easier from here."

James felt a knot form in his stomach. The mission had been successful, but Walker's words made it clear: this was just the beginning.

There were more targets, more dangers, and more choices to make. It wasn't going to get any better.

"We've got a few days of downtime. Use it wisely," Walker continued. "Rest up, reload, and prepare for what comes next. We'll be heading out again soon."

The team dispersed, but James stayed in his seat, his eyes focused on the table. He couldn't shake the feeling that something was coming. Something bigger than anything they had faced so far.

Nathan sat next to him, reading his expression.

"You alright?" he asked quietly.

James nodded, though the truth was, he wasn't. He wasn't sure if he would ever be again.

"We'll get through this," Nathan said, as if reading his thoughts. "Together."

James wasn't sure if that would be enough. But for now, it was the only thing he had to hold on to.

The death of Private Harris weighed heavily on the platoon. The young soldier had been a bright, enthusiastic member of the unit, and his loss was a reminder of the harsh realities they faced. The survivors had to carry on, but the grief hung over them like a cloud.

James found himself thinking about the families back home. The mothers, fathers, sisters, and brothers who would never see their loved ones again.

Every time a soldier died, it wasn't just a statistic, it was a life. A person with hopes, dreams, and a future that had been cut short.And then there was the guilt.

Was there something they could have done differently? Could they have saved Harris?

Nathan had tried to keep morale high, but even he was visibly affected.

There was no easy way to process the pain, and there was no escaping the reality that war claimed lives, both the enemy's and their own.

But they pressed on. The mission wasn't over. The enemy hadn't been defeated, and there was still work to be done. The soldiers had learned to compartmentalise their emotions, to push the grief aside and focus on the next objective.

But deep down, they all knew that the cost of war was far greater than any of them could truly understand.

The days after Harris's death were a blur. Each mission bled into the next, the fatigue creeping into their bones as they pushed through the gruelling heat of the desert.

James had never known the kind of exhaustion that felt like it might break him, but now, it was a constant presence.

His muscles ached, his mind fogged, and yet, he kept going. It was what soldiers did.

Nathan had become quieter in the wake of Harris's death, though his leadership never faltered.

He kept the platoon moving forward, giving orders with the same sharp precision that had earned him the respect of his soldiers. But James could see it in his eyes, the toll it was taking. The pain of watching young men die. Of feeling like there was always more to lose.

They were given a few days to rest at base after the firefight, but it felt like the quiet was almost more suffocating than the battle.

The soldiers sat in their tents, nursing wounds, both physical and emotional, and trying to find distractions. Some wrote letters home, some played cards, while others, like Marco, took long walks alone, no one asking where he went.

James found himself alone on a small hilltop, looking out over the base. The horizon was a jagged line of mountains, the sky painted with the soft colours of a fading sunset.

It should have been peaceful, but all he could think about was Harris.

He could still see his face, still hear his voice, laughing at some stupid joke in the mess hall just hours before the ambush. Now, he was just another name on the casualty list.

A familiar voice interrupted his thoughts.

"Don't stay out here too long. The sun sets fast around here."

James turned to see Nathan standing a few feet away, his silhouette framed against the colourful sky. Despite everything, he still exuded that quiet confidence.

"I'm fine," James replied, trying to shake off the heaviness in his chest. "Just needed a minute."

Nathan nodded, walking over to join him. They both sat in silence, the weight of the moment hanging between them.

"You know," Nathan began, after a long pause, "I didn't always want to be here. I never imagined I'd be a lifer, a guy who's seen more combat than most people see in a lifetime.

But sometimes, you end up where you are, not because you planned it, but because it's the only place left. I guess it's just part of the job."

James glanced over at him. "Doesn't make it easier, though, does it?"

"No." Nathan's voice was steady but raw. "It doesn't. But you get used to it. You learn to live with it, and eventually, you come to terms with what it means to be a soldier."

James swallowed hard. "I don't think I'm ever going to get used to it. I don't know if I want to."

Nathan gave him a somber smile. "No one ever does. But that's why you've got the guy next to you. That's why you trust your team. It's the only way to keep going."

James didn't have a response. He just stared at the setting sun, the weight of his thoughts pressing down harder. He could feel the burden of war taking root in his mind, twisting and pulling at his sanity. He wondered how long it would be before it became too much to bear.

The days that followed were some of the hardest James had faced. They went on mission after mission, always moving through the same dust choked streets, always ready for the next attack. But the physical toll was only one part of the war. The mental strain was another beast entirely.

James had seen the signs of PTSD starting to take hold in his comrades. Marco had become more withdrawn, his usual calm demeanour shifting to something darker.

He didn't speak much anymore, preferring solitude, his eyes constantly scanning the horizon, as if he were always waiting for the next battle.

Nathan, too, seemed on edge. The long hours, the loss, the constant threat of danger, he was no longer the same man who had led them in the early days of training.

James could see the exhaustion in his eyes, the weariness in his movements. But Nathan, ever the leader, didn't show it. Not to the soldiers, not to anyone else.

The weight of leadership had a way of crushing a person, and James couldn't help but wonder if Nathan would crack under it eventually.

One afternoon, during a rare moment of downtime, James sat with Marco near the back of the base. The older soldier had finally opened up about something personal. It wasn't much, but it was more than James had heard from him in weeks.

"You know," Marco said, staring down at the dusty ground, "when I first joined the army, it was different. I had a family at home, a wife and two kids.

I thought I could protect them, make a difference. I thought… I thought I was doing the right thing. But you start to see how everything changes, how the world gets a little smaller with every person you lose."

James nodded, unsure what to say. Marco's words hit close to home. He thought about his own family, his mother, his sister, and how different his life had been before the army. Before the war.

"Do you ever wish you hadn't come?" James asked.

Marco took a long time to answer. "Sometimes. But we don't have that luxury. We don't get to choose, not when you're in it. I've seen things… things that stay with you. You can't just walk away from it. But you keep going. Because that's all we can do. You push through, for them, for us, for the ones who didn't make it."

James stared at the ground, thinking about Marco's words. It was a harsh reality, one that he was beginning to understand all too well.

The weight of war wasn't something that could be explained in a single conversation? It was something you carried with you, day in and day out, until it became part of who you were.

Chapter 6 The Long Road Home

The end of their deployment was finally approaching. The soldiers had endured months of combat, of loss, of survival. They had pushed through every obstacle that came their way, and now, it seemed, there was an end in sight.

But even as they prepared to leave the conflict zone, James couldn't shake the feeling that something was missing. The war had taken so much from them. It had shaped them into something they hadn't been before. And no matter how hard they tried, there was no going back to the people they had once been.

As they boarded the plane back home, James couldn't help but glance around at his fellow soldiers. Marco sat quietly, his eyes staring out the window. Nathan, as always, remained stoic, though there was a far off look in his eyes, as if he were already preparing for what came next.

The camaraderie that had once been so strong now felt fragile, broken in ways that words couldn't describe.

Back home, they would have to learn how to live again.

The weight of war might have been left behind in the desert, but the scars would remain. For all of them.

James looked out the window, watching the landscape below. He didn't know what his future held. He didn't know if he could ever truly find peace again.

But one thing was certain: he had survived. And that, in itself, was a victory.

Years later, James would still think about the war. He would think about the soldiers who never made it home, about the families torn apart, and about the lessons learned in the harshest of conditions.

But he would also think about the bond they had shared, the way they had looked out for one another, even when everything around them was falling apart.

He would think about how, in the end, it wasn't just about fighting the enemy, it was about fighting for each other.

And, as he stood on the edge of a new chapter in his life, James would realise that he had become something more than he ever thought possible: a soldier, yes, but more importantly, a man who had learned the true meaning of sacrifice, of duty, and of courage.

It had been months since James returned home, yet the memories of the war still lingered. He had tried to move on, tried to bury the images of the battlefield deep within himself, but they crept back in at the most unexpected times, during quiet moments, at night when sleep wouldn't come, or when he least expected it.

The harsh sounds of gunfire, the faces of the fallen, the weight of the decisions made, it was all there, haunting him in ways he didn't know how to explain.

Home felt like a foreign place. His mother, who had once welcomed him with open arms, was now a stranger in her own right. She couldn't understand why he was so different, why he no longer smiled when he heard the sound of her laughter. His friends, too, had changed.

They tried to fill the silence with stories from their own lives, but none of it seemed to matter to James anymore. The world felt distant, disconnected from the person he had become in the wake of the war.

He had tried to go back to school, to resume his life as if nothing had happened, but it was impossible.

Every classroom felt like a cage, every interaction a reminder of what he had left behind. He couldn't focus on the trivialities of homework or the small talk of acquaintances when his mind kept returning to the things he had witnessed, the lives lost, the choices made, the weight of it all.

The worst part was the loneliness. He wasn't alone physically; his mother, his old friends, even a few soldiers from his platoon had reached out.

But the isolation he felt was profound. It was as if a wall had been erected between him and the world, a barrier no one could cross. No one could truly understand what it was like.

Nathan had tried calling him a few times, but James didn't answer. Marco had written him once, a short letter that read more like an afterthought. The war had taken its toll on them all, and they were scattered, each dealing with it in their own way.

Nathan, in particular, seemed like he was struggling. He had gone silent, disappearing from everyone's radar for weeks at a time. No one knew where he had gone, but James could guess.

It was late one evening when James got a call from an unfamiliar number. His gut twisted as he reached for the phone, unsure of what to expect.

"Hello?" he answered cautiously.

There was a long pause at the other end before a familiar voice broke through.

"Monroe… it's Nathan."

James's heart skipped a beat. "Nathan?" His voice cracked slightly. He hadn't heard from him in weeks. "Where have you been? Everyone's been worried."

"I… I know. I've been… working through some things. You know how it is. The war… it doesn't just end when you come home. Not really."

James felt a pang of guilt for not reaching out sooner. He had been avoiding his former platoon members, feeling as though he didn't have the strength to talk to them, to admit that he wasn't okay. "Yeah, I get it. But Nathan, you've been gone for so long. What's going on? Are you okay?"

There was a long sigh on the other end of the line. "Honestly, Monroe, I don't know. I thought I'd be able to move on after all this time, but I'm not sure that I can. Sometimes I feel like I'm losing myself. It's hard, you know? To let go of everything.

The mission, the men we lost. I keep hearing their voices, and it's like they're right behind me. I don't know how to shake it. I don't know how to move on."

James's throat tightened, and for a moment, he didn't know what to say. He understood better than anyone the weight Nathan was carrying. But they hadn't been prepared for this. They hadn't been taught how to return from war, how to heal the wounds it left on the inside.

"I feel the same way," James said softly. "I've tried. I've tried so hard to just live like everything's normal. But I can't. I'm not the same person. None of us are."

There was silence between them, and James imagined Nathan sitting alone in some dimly lit room, the same isolation gnawing at him. He could hear the faint sound of Nathan's breath on the other end, and it was the only sound he needed to understand.

They were both still fighting, even though the war was technically over. The war inside was still ongoing, and there was no clear end in sight.

"I don't know how to do this anymore, Nathan," James admitted, the words feeling like they had been trapped inside him for far too long. "I don't know how to live with this. With all of it. The guilt, the anger, the fear… it's like I'm losing myself too."

Nathan's voice was low but steady. "You're not alone, Monroe. We're all in this together, even if it doesn't feel that way. We just have to figure out how to keep moving forward. One step at a time."

James closed his eyes and nodded, though Nathan couldn't see him. They weren't alone, he reminded himself. The soldiers who had fought beside him, who had shared those unbearable moments of pain and loss, were still there. He wasn't alone, even if it felt like it.

"I'm here, Nathan. Whenever you're ready to talk. We all need to get through this together."

Nathan paused, then quietly responded, "Thanks, Monroe. I think I needed to hear that."

The conversation ended shortly after that, and James sat in silence for a long time, his phone resting in his lap. The weight of Nathan's words, and the weight of his own, lingered in the air. It felt like a small, fragile bridge had been built between them, one that wasn't going to fix everything, but at least it was a start.

The next few days were quiet. James didn't reach out to anyone else, but he thought a lot about the conversation he'd had with Nathan. It reminded him of the bond they had shared during the deployment, the way they had relied on each other, not just for survival, but for some semblance of humanity in the face of everything they had gone through.

The war had been brutal, but it hadn't just been about the enemy. It had been about their camaraderie, about the way they had each carried the other through the worst of it.

He realised, as he sat in the stillness of his apartment, that the war had changed them, but it didn't have to define them forever. He wasn't sure how to move forward, but he knew that holding on to the past wasn't going to help. He had to find a way to rebuild, not just his life, but himself.

A few weeks later, James did something he hadn't thought he'd be able to do. He picked up the phone again, this time dialling Marco's number. It rang a few times before he heard his friend's voice at the other end.

"Monroe?" Marco sounded surprised, but not in a bad way. "You okay?"

"I've been better," James admitted. "But I think I'm getting there. I just… I wanted to check in. How are you?"

"Surviving, man," Marco replied, his tone lighter than James had expected. "You know how it is. Some days are better than others."

There was a long pause before Marco added, "I get it. We all do. We just need to find a way to make peace with it, somehow."

James nodded, even though Marco couldn't see him. It felt like there was something new between them now, something less heavy but more honest. They didn't have all the answers, and maybe they never would. But they had each other. And for now, that was enough.

"I've been thinking," James said after a while. "Maybe it's time we all got together. You, me, Nathan… everyone from the unit. I don't know.

Maybe it's time we try to heal, to get out of our heads and stop hiding."

There was a brief silence on the other end. Then Marco's voice, softer than before, spoke up.

"I think that's a good idea. We could all use a little bit of that."

The conversation ended soon after, but James felt lighter. Maybe it won't be easy. Maybe they will all carry their scars for the rest of their lives. But they weren't alone in this. They had never been. And perhaps that, in itself, was the key to moving forward.

In the days that followed, the group of soldiers began to reconnect, tentatively at first, sharing stories, asking about one another's lives, and trying, in their own way, to find the pieces of themselves they had lost. It wasn't a quick fix.

There were still bad days, still moments when the past came crashing back, still times when the silence was overwhelming. But there were also moments of understanding, of real, unspoken solidarity that only those who had been through the same hell could truly grasp.

Months passed. Life slowly returned to a new kind of normal, though James was still learning to navigate it.

He wasn't the person he had been before the war. He wasn't the same as he had been during it either. But he was learning. One day at a time. One step at a time.

And when he thought back to that plane ride home, the uncertainty he had felt about the future, he realised something important: surviving wasn't just about enduring the battle.

 It was about finding the courage to face what came after. It was about living with what had happened and deciding, despite everything, that he was still going to move forward.

No, it hadn't been easy. But James survived the war. And now, he was going to survive life.

As the months passed, James began to carve out a new existence, though it often felt like walking through a fog. His days were filled with routine: work, gym sessions, visits with his mother, but the nights were still a battle.

He didn't always sleep, and when he did, the dreams were sometimes more vivid than he could handle.

Faces from the war, explosions, the sound of gunfire ringing in his ears, the feeling of being trapped in the chaos.

But in the quiet moments, when the weight of the world felt too heavy, he reminded himself that progress wasn't linear. Healing wasn't something that could be checked off a list.

He found solace in the smaller things. The quiet comfort of reading a book without the weight of an SA80 on his shoulder. The feeling of grass beneath his bare feet as he took long walks around his neighbourhood, the hum of normal life settling into his chest like an unfamiliar rhythm. Sometimes, he would walk past the local coffee shop where he had once spent hours with friends before everything changed.

It was strange how something so simple could feel like such a big thing now. He no longer felt like an outsider there, though the familiar faces still made him pause, as if wondering whether he belonged in that world anymore.

It was during one of these walks that he received a text from Marco.

We're doing a reunion, a small one. You in?

It took James a few seconds to process. A reunion. The old unit. For the first time, the thought didn't scare him.

There was a part of him that had been avoiding them, afraid of the pain that might come with seeing them again, of facing everything they had been through together, but now, something inside him shifted. Maybe this was exactly what they needed.

Yeah. I'll be there.

A few weeks later, James found himself at a small bar, standing outside with Nathan and Marco. The others from their unit had arrived earlier, their laughter already spilling out into the street as they reunited. It felt strange, almost surreal, seeing them all together again.

They hadn't been in the same room since their return. There have been attempts at reaching out, but nothing like this.

The weight of the unspoken hung in the air, but it was different now, less suffocating.

Nathan, ever the Stoic leader, was the first to greet James with a handshake. His eyes were tired, but there was something lighter about him. "You made it," he said with a small smile.

"Yeah. I guess I did," James replied, his voice steady but carrying the hint of emotion he couldn't quite suppress.

It was good to see them all again. For a moment, the world felt normal.

The others were just as welcoming, though there was an unspoken understanding that the things they'd gone through would never leave them. They didn't have to explain what they had seen, what they had felt.

There was no need to tell stories of sacrifice or survival. They were all survivors now, each one of them marked by the war, but still here. Still alive.

Over the next few hours, the group shared laughs and stories, reminiscing about the good times they'd had together during their deployment. It wasn't all about the war.

They spoke of mundane things, old jokes that never got old, drunken nights in base camps, the ridiculousness of some of their training exercises. They talked about life after the military, the challenges, the surprises. It wasn't perfect, but it was real.

It was when the conversation slowed, and the room quieted, that James felt a pang in his chest. They were all together, but the absence of the ones who hadn't made it back was palpable. Private Harris. Corporal Steele. The soldiers they had lost in the chaos. The weight of those names hung between them like a shadow.

Marco was the first to break the silence. "We've all changed," he said quietly, looking around the table at the men who had been through hell and back. "But we're still here. And that's something."

The group nodded in agreement. It wasn't just survival that mattered, it was what they made of the pieces they had left.

James glanced over at Nathan, who gave him a silent nod. He didn't need to say anything. Nathan had been through the darkest parts of this journey with him, and James knew that, no matter what, they would continue to stand by each other.

The conversation drifted into silence once again, but this time, it wasn't uncomfortable. It was the kind of quiet that comes with understanding, with shared experience. The kind of quiet where no words were necessary.

For James, that was when he realised something important: he wasn't alone.

The war had taken so much from him, but it had also given him something, brothers. Not just soldiers he had served with, but friends who truly understood.

And though the road ahead was uncertain, and though the scars would never fully fade, he knew he wasn't walking it alone anymore.

He had his brothers, and together, they would figure it out.

He looked around at the men who had become a family, each of them broken in their own way, but still standing. And for the first time in a long time, James felt the faint stirrings of peace. It wouldn't come all at once. It never did. But he knew this was a step in the right direction.

The night ended quietly, with the group parting ways, their bonds a little stronger, the weight of their shared history a little lighter.

The months that followed the reunion felt like a strange mix of progress and setbacks.

James had thought that reconnecting with his brothers would provide the healing he so desperately needed, but the truth was, the wounds from war ran deep, and they didn't just vanish because of a few shared laughs and familiar faces.

Every night, James found himself waking in a cold sweat, his heart pounding in his chest.

The shadows in his room sometimes seemed to shift, taking on the forms of things he couldn't explain: an enemy soldier, a faceless figure, someone reaching for him.

The sound of distant explosions echoed in his ears, and for a moment, he was back there, back in the thick of it. His breath would catch in his throat, his hands shaking as he tried to force himself back to reality.

He knew the term for it, PTSD. He had heard it before, in the briefings, in the hospital rooms. He had even seen it in the eyes of some of his fellow soldiers. But to experience it? That was different. It was something that couldn't be fully understood unless you lived it. And now, James was living it.

He had tried to bury the feelings. He told himself he was fine, told others he was fine. He tried to carry on, go back to normal life. But the truth was, nothing felt normal.

The anxiety, the irritability, the difficulty sleeping, the overwhelming sense of dread it all lingered in the background, threatening to pull him under whenever he let his guard down.

At work, he found himself snapping at people over small things. He didn't mean to, but the pressure built up in his chest like a ticking time bomb. He couldn't explain why he was irritable, why the constant noise of people talking in the background felt like a weight on his shoulders.

He'd isolate himself in the corner of the office, his mind far away from the spreadsheets and reports he was supposed to be working on. He hated how the silence in his head was often interrupted by memories of war.

He started avoiding crowded places, bars, shopping malls, even public transportation. The loud noises, the crowds of people, the feeling of being trapped, it all triggered the anxiety that he couldn't seem to control. He couldn't explain it to anyone, because no one truly understood.

Even Marco and Nathan, despite their own

experiences, couldn't understand the depth of what he was feeling. Not anymore.

His mother noticed the changes. James hadn't been back to visit her much since he returned. He wasn't sure what it was, whether it was the guilt he felt for not being there when she needed him or the sense of alienation that had grown between them, but every time she tried to talk to him, the conversation always felt stilted, awkward.

Like they were strangers, unable to bridge the gap between the son she once knew and the man he had become.

"James," she asked one evening, her voice quiet, "are you okay? You've been so distant lately. You don't seem like yourself."

He had tried to force a smile, but the truth was, he wasn't okay. He was far from it. "I'm fine, Mom," he said, his voice tight. "Just… tired. You know, work stuff."

But his mother knew better.

She had seen him grow up, seen him leave for basic training, and now, she saw the man who had come back from war, someone different.

The fear in her eyes was hard to ignore, but James didn't have the words to explain himself. Not yet. Maybe not ever.

As time went on, James started to slip further away from everyone, including himself. The constant weight of guilt pressed down on him, guilt for being alive when so many others weren't, guilt for the things he had done, for the choices that still haunted him.

He couldn't shake the thought that maybe he could have done more. Maybe he could have saved the others. The memories of Harris, Steele, and the others who didn't come back, the ones who had never made it to the plane, always loomed over him like ghosts. He could still see their faces, still hear their last words.

One night, after a long shift at work, James found himself sitting on the edge of his bed, staring at the wall. The room felt suffocating, the walls closing in on him. He couldn't breathe.

His heart was racing, the familiar rush of panic beginning to claw its way to the surface.

The memories flooded in. The gunfire, the blood, the sounds of men screaming, and the silence that followed.

"Focus, Monroe," he whispered to himself, his hands shaking as he tried to centre himself.

He had learned breathing exercises in therapy, but it never seemed to work when it hit him hard. He tried counting, tried focusing on the feeling of the bed beneath him, but the images didn't go away.

In the dead of the night, the guilt and pain overwhelmed him, and for the first time, he broke.

He had spent so long pretending to be fine, pretending to have control, but now, sitting alone in the dark, he realised he had been lying to himself. His chest heaved with silent sobs. He wasn't fine. He was far from it.

The next morning, he knew something had to change. He couldn't keep living like this, trapped in his own mind, isolated from everyone. But reaching out was hard. Admitting he needed help was harder than any combat mission he had ever faced.

He remembered Nathan's voice from months ago, when they had first opened up to each other. "We're in this together." It was a promise. But right now, James wasn't sure if he believed it.

Still, something in him stirred. Maybe it wasn't about fighting this battle alone. Maybe the path to healing wasn't through isolation, but through connection, through reaching out to the ones who had shared the same pain.

James sat at his kitchen table, staring at his phone. He scrolled through his contacts and found Nathan's number. The hesitation lingered in his fingertips, but he couldn't keep pretending anymore. He needed to talk to someone who would understand. So, with a deep breath, he hit send.

"Nathan, you still around? I think I need to talk."

Within seconds, Nathan replied: "Always, man. You're not alone."

And for the first time in a long time, James allowed himself to believe it. Maybe the road ahead would be long, maybe the scars would never fade completely, but reaching out connecting with those who understood was the first real step toward healing. And for now, that was enough.

And as James walked home, the stars overhead feeling just a little bit closer, he realised that maybe, just maybe, he could finally breathe again.

CHAPTER 7 REBUILDING THE PIECES

Over the next few months, James slowly began to find his way back. He started attending therapy something he had resisted for a long time. At first, it felt awkward, speaking about his experiences to someone who hadn't lived them. But gradually, he began to make progress.

He talked about Harris's death, about the lives he had taken, the weight of leadership, and the memories that kept him awake at night. He cried. He yelled. He let the emotions he had buried for so long spill out in front of someone who listened without judgment.

Nathan had returned to base and reconnected with the others. Despite time and distance, their bond, forged in the fire of war, remained unbroken. It wasn't easy, but they were learning. Learning to live with their demons. Learning that healing isn't linear. That it takes time, and that sometimes, time is the hardest part.

James still carried the faces of the fallen with him. The decisions he had made still replayed in his mind. But the sharp pain had dulled. He was no longer drowning.

Instead, he carried the pain like a shadow always there, but no longer all-consuming.

As the months passed, the soldier within him, the man who had fought and sacrificed, began to make peace with the man he had become. He realised the road ahead would not be easy, but he had a choice: be consumed by the past, or build a future from its remnants.

He wasn't sure what that future looked like, but he knew one thing, he wasn't alone. And that made all the difference.

The war may have ended, but the real battle had just begun. The battle for peace, within himself, and with the men who had fought beside him, was a long, uncertain road. But James was no longer afraid to walk it.

Years later, James would look back on that time with a sense of both loss and growth. The war had left its mark, but it had also shaped him into someone who understood the value of resilience, of friendship, and of moving forward, no matter how hard the road.

The scars, both visible and invisible, would always be there. They were reminders of the price paid. But as he looked around at those who had helped him endure, he understood something vital:

They had survived together. And together, they would continue to rebuild, one day at a time.

In time, James found a rhythm in his life. It wasn't perfect, but it was a life. He attended therapy regularly, though there were still days when the memories felt heavy, too much to carry.

He began working with other veterans, helping them transition back into civilian life. It wasn't grand, but it gave him purpose, something steady to hold onto.

Nathan, Marco, and the rest of the platoon drifted in and out of his life. They stayed in touch, in small, quiet ways. Over the years, they'd learned that recovery didn't come from heroic comebacks or dramatic declarations. It came from showing up. From taking each step, no matter how small. From reminding each other they weren't alone.

The hardest part was always the silence.

Even with his team, even with support, there were days when the quiet settled around him like a weight. The empty spaces felt endless. The war hadn't just taken lives, it had taken parts of himself. Pieces he hadn't even known were missing until they were gone.

For a long time, he avoided relationships. He couldn't imagine being vulnerable, being seen by someone who might notice the scars beneath the surface. The ones no one ever talked about.

But life, in its quiet persistence, moved forward.

One day, he met someone, Sarah. She had her own battles, her own history. She didn't push him. She didn't demand answers to questions he wasn't ready to face. Slowly, patiently, they built something together.

It wasn't perfect, but it was real.

Through her, James began to understand that healing didn't mean forgetting. It meant making space for the past. Finding room beside it for the things he was learning to love.

It had been five years since James last visited the cemetery.

Harris. And a few Others from the unit. Had been laid to rest in neat rows of stone. The cemetery had always been a weight he carried, a place he avoided, because going back meant facing everything he tried to bury.

But on this day, something shifted.

He found himself driving down the long, winding road to the cemetery gates. The sky was grey, the air sharp with the promise of winter. His hands were tight on the wheel. He

hadn't told Sarah. He hadn't told anyone. This was something he needed to do alone.

He walked among the graves in silence. The years felt heavy on his shoulders. He saw their faces in his mind, Harris's laugh, Marco's steady gaze, Nathan's quiet strength. They were still with him, always had been, alive in memory if not in body.

He stopped at Harris's grave, crouched beside the cold stone.

"I'm sorry," he whispered. "I wish I could've done more. I wish I could've kept you safe."

The wind rustled the leaves in the trees. For a long moment, James just sat there. Silent. Letting the grief come.

He didn't expect an answer. He didn't believe in signs anymore. Only the stillness remained, the kind that holds both sorrow and peace in its embrace.

Eventually, James stood. He wiped his eyes and took a breath.

It wasn't about closure. He had long stopped believing in such things. The past didn't tie itself into neat conclusions. It lingered. It became a part of who you are.

What mattered was what he did with it.

As he walked away from the cemetery, he didn't know if peace was truly possible but he knew survival meant something. And he wasn't walking alone anymore.

Some days were easier than others. On the good days, James could get out of bed without the weight pressing down on his chest. He'd make coffee, walk the dog he never thought he'd own, and sit in the early morning stillness, watching the world come to life.

On the bad days, the war felt closer. It wasn't in explosions or flashbacks, it was in the quiet. In the clatter of a dropped spoon that made him flinch. In the empty chair across from him at the kitchen table. In the sudden moments of stillness that reminded him of waiting for something to go wrong.

He kept a journal, at his therapist's suggestion. At first, he hated it. What was the point of writing it down? But then the pages started to fill with things he hadn't said out loud. He wrote letters to Harris. To the men who never came back. He wrote about the fear, the guilt, the small, quiet moments of peace that came when he least expected them.

There was one entry he returned to often:

"You're not here, but I still talk to you. I think about what we'd be doing if you had made it back. Would you have married your girl? Would you have hated civilian life like the rest of us? Would we still sit in silence over pints, not needing to say a thing? I miss that. I miss you. I'm trying to be okay. I hope that's enough."

Sometimes, that was all he could manage.

Working with other veterans brought a strange kind of healing. They didn't need to explain things to each other. They all knew the look, the weight behind the eyes, the stiffness in the shoulders. James didn't try to fix anyone. He just showed up. Listened. Let them talk or not talk. Sometimes, that was all that was needed.

He spoke at a small memorial one evening, standing in front of a crowd of families, old comrades, and wide-eyed young recruits who hadn't yet seen what war could take.

"I used to think strength meant not feeling anything. That grief was weakness. But I've learned that carrying pain and still choosing to live, that's strength. We don't move on.

We carry on. That's what we do."

It wasn't poetic. But it was real. And afterward, a mother who had lost her son came up and quietly took his hand. She didn't say anything. She didn't need to.

Later that year, Sarah found James sitting alone on the back porch, staring into the fading dusk.

She sat beside him and took his hand. "You've been quiet lately."

"I went back to the cemetery again," he said.

"Did it help?"

"I don't know," he admitted. "But it didn't hurt as much."

Sarah rested her head on his shoulder. "That's something." They sat in silence, watching the light fade. And in that moment, surrounded by the quiet hum of life continuing, James felt something close to peace.

Not perfect. Not complete.

But enough.

CHAPTER 8 NEW BEGINNING

The years after that day at the cemetery brought new changes. James and Sarah moved in together, slowly, at first, but eventually with the kind of stability he hadn't known since before the war.

They didn't talk about the past much. Sarah knew about it, of course. She had seen the subtle signs, the moments when he would withdraw into himself, when the nightmares would come back, but she never pushed him. Instead, she let him speak when he was ready, and that patience made all the difference.

James had started working with a nonprofit organisation that helped veterans transition back into civilian life. It felt like a fitting purpose, something that connected him to others who understood the struggle, but it also gave him a way to pay forward the support he had received over the years.

He worked with men and women who had faced the same battles, and together, they shared their stories, sometimes without words, and found new ways to move forward.

Nathan, too, had made progress. He had opened up about his struggles in a way he never had before, and he began

working with soldiers who were just coming home. The two of them had reconnected over the years, their bond slowly mending, one conversation at a time.

They never talked about the war much, at least, not in detail. But it was enough to know that they were there for each other, that they understood the depth of what had been lost and what had been survived.

James still thought about Marco, about his quiet wisdom and the way he had carried the burden of leadership with such grace. Marco had found peace, though in his own way. He had remarried and had children, but the shadow of the war still lingered in his eyes. It always would.

The scars of the past will never completely fade. They never do. But as James looked ahead, he saw that the road he had traveled, though long and hard, had brought him to a place of understanding.

He had learned that the weight of war, of loss, wasn't something that could be erased or forgotten.

But it was something that could be carried, something that could be woven into the fabric of life, into the story of who he had become.

And in that story, there was room for healing, for hope, for the quiet understanding that survival wasn't just about living, it was about learning to live with what had been lost and finding strength in the face of it.

James didn't have all the answers. He didn't know what tomorrow would bring. But he knew this: he wasn't alone. Not anymore. The men he had fought beside, the women who loved him, the soldiers who had walked through hell and come back. Together, they had rebuilt their lives, piece by piece. And they would keep rebuilding, for as long as it took.

The road was still long, but it was one he was no longer afraid to walk.

Years passed with a gradual sense of normalcy. It wasn't perfect, but it was progress.
The noise of the past, gunfire, explosions, the constant hum of fear and survival had faded into the background. In its place, a quieter, more peaceful life had taken root. James woke each morning, went to work, and spent evenings with Sarah.

They had a routine, something steady, something that felt real. But every so often, the past will resurface.

He still had his moments of darkness. Sometimes, late at night, he'd wake up with the weight of something pressing on his chest, a reminder of the ghosts that still followed him.

Other times, the sound of a distant car backfiring or a sudden loud noise would make his heart race, sending him back to the battlefields, if only for a moment. He would lie there in the dark, fighting the urge to react, to grab for a weapon that wasn't there. But Sarah, always patient, would gently place her hand on his arm, offering a wordless reminder that he was home.

And slowly, he would ground himself in the present. In her. In the life they had built.

One spring morning, James stood at the back of a small hall, watching a group of young veterans speak on a panel he'd helped organise. The room was modest, but packed, families, soldiers, even local leaders had come to listen.

He didn't speak that day. He didn't need to. Watching those men and women share their struggles, their triumphs, the raw honesty of it all, it was enough. That was the mission now: not to save anyone, but to remind them they weren't broken beyond repair.

Later, someone approached him, barely twenty, fresh out of service, eyes full of questions and fear. James listened as the young man tried to explain what it felt like to be home but not here.

"I don't know who I'm supposed to be anymore," he said.

James put a hand on his shoulder. "None of us did. But you don't have to figure it out alone."

It wasn't profound. It was simple. But the young man nodded, and for the first time that day, his shoulders eased just a little.

At home, life continued in quiet rhythms. Sarah began taking photography classes, something she'd always wanted to do. James would sometimes find her in the garden, capturing the soft gold of sunset filtering through the trees, or the quiet strength in an old veteran's hands during a gathering.

He loved her for it, for the way she saw beauty in the things others overlooked. In him, most of all.

They talked, some nights, about what the future might hold. Children, maybe. A small cottage somewhere quieter. Nothing was certain, but for James, the idea of a future was something he hadn't dared to believe in for a long time. Now, it felt possible.

Not perfect. Not easy. But possible.

On the anniversary of Harris's death, James returned to the cemetery, not out of obligation, but because he wanted to. He brought a folded photo Sarah had taken of their team, years ago, during one of their rare lighthearted moments, mud-caked, exhausted, laughing like kids.

He tucked it beneath the gravestone.

"I miss you," he said quietly. "But I think you'd be proud. We're still here. Still fighting for peace this time."

The wind whispered through the trees, and for a moment, James swore he could hear humming.

Later that afternoon, James received a letter from Nathan. It had been a while since they had caught up, and the message was simple, yet it made his heart quicken in a way that was both comforting and unsettling:

"Monroe, I've been thinking about the past lately. I know we don't talk about it much, but I think it's time we did. I'm organising something, just us. A reunion.

The guys. I don't know if it'll be easy, but it might help. What do you say?"

It wasn't a surprise. Nathan had always been a leader, even now. And though he was often quiet, there was a part of him that still carried the weight of responsibility for the men he'd led.

It had been years since they'd all been together in the same place, and James had to admit the thought of reconnecting with the others, of sharing their stories, both terrified and comforted him. But the more he thought about it, the more he realised it was something he needed to do.

The reunion took place at a small cabin in the woods, far away from the city, surrounded by trees and the stillness of nature. Nathan had organised it meticulously, everyone was invited. It was supposed to be an opportunity to remember their fallen comrades, to laugh, to cry, and to, perhaps, find some kind of peace.

When James arrived, he saw the familiar faces of his brothers in arms, but they weren't the same men he had fought alongside years ago.

They were older, their faces etched with the marks of time and experience. Some of them had families now, some were still carrying scars, both visible and invisible, that told the stories of the war they had all survived.

"Monroe," Nathan said with a smile as James stepped out of the car.

He still had the same quiet strength in his eyes, but there was something different now, an openness, a willingness to let others in. "Good to see you, man."

"Good to be here," James replied, shaking his hand. "It's been a long time."

Inside the cabin, the group had already started to gather. Marco was there, looking just as steady and unshakable as always. He had settled into a quieter life after the war, becoming a counsel or to fellow veterans. But there was a weariness in his eyes, a reminder of the ghosts he carried too.

They sat around the table, and for a while, the conversation flowed easily. They reminisced about old times, telling stories of training, of missions, of the jokes they had shared in the midst of battle.

It was a welcome distraction, and James felt the weight of the past lifting just a little, bit by bit. But as the night wore on, the conversation shifted. It always did.

Marco spoke first. "I know we don't talk about it much, but I think we need to. We've all been through something together, and it's not just something you can leave behind. I know I tried. I tried to be 'normal,' but it didn't work like that."

There was a collective silence as everyone nodded in agreement. It was true. The war had shaped them, changed them in ways they could never explain to anyone who hadn't been there.

Nathan took a deep breath, his voice quieter than usual. "It's okay to talk about it now. We've all been carrying these things alone for too long. We need to heal together. So let's share it."

One by one, each man spoke. They spoke of their losses, the men who hadn't made it home, the faces that still haunted their dreams.

They spoke of the guilt, the fear, and the nights they had spent lying awake, unsure if they could ever move forward. Some cried, some didn't. But they all understood. They all felt the weight of it, even as they spoke the words they had been too afraid to say for so long.

James found himself talking too. He spoke about Harris, about the ambush, about the moments when everything felt like it was spinning out of control. He spoke about the burden of leadership that Nathan had carried, the way Marco had quietly supported them all, even when he had his own battles to face.

And he spoke about how, for so long, he hadn't known how to be anything other than a soldier. He didn't know how to be himself.

When it was his turn, Nathan turned to him, his eyes intense but kind. "You've come a long way, Monroe. You've been through a lot. I think we all have. But you're not alone. We're all in this together."

The reunion was a turning point for James. It wasn't magic. It wasn't some instant cure all that fixed everything. But it was the beginning of something.

They had finally, truly faced the war together, not as soldiers in combat, but as men who had shared something that would always be a part of them.

As the weekend wore on, the stories of the past were told and retold. Laughter and tears filled the air. And by the time they said their goodbyes, there was a sense of quiet understanding among them. They weren't just soldiers anymore. They were survivors. And in that survival, they had found a new way to be.

James left the cabin with a sense of peace that had eluded him for so long. He wasn't fixed, not in the way he once imagined he would be. But he was stronger. The burden of the past had lightened, and he no longer carried it alone.

CHAPTER 9 MOVING FORWARD TOGETHER

Back home, life continued. James and Sarah had begun planning their future. There was talk of getting married, of starting a family. It was a future he hadn't dared to dream of for a long time. But now, with each passing day, he felt the possibility of it.

Nathan, Marco, and the others were always there, present in ways that James had never expected. They kept in touch, shared stories, and supported each other through the struggles that remained. They were no longer just a group of men who had fought a war together. They were a family.

And though the scars remained, the pain, too, had become a part of who they were, a part of their shared history. But James had learned that healing wasn't about erasing the past. It was about learning to live with it, about finding strength in the stories they had shared and the bond they had formed.

Years later, James would return to that cabin.

The reunion was no longer a onetime thing, it had become a tradition, a yearly reminder that the past would always be with them, but it didn't have to define them.

As James stood on the porch, looking out at the forest, he realised that the legacy of the fallen was not just in the memories, the pain, and the losses. It was also in the way they had rebuilt, the way they had lived, loved, and carried forward.

Together.

It had been nearly a decade since the war had ended, and James often found himself reflecting on how much had changed. In some ways, it felt like a lifetime ago. He had settled into a new rhythm, one that, although not perfect, was filled with more moments of peace than turmoil.

But there were still times when the weight of the past would suddenly fall on him like a thick fog. Moments when the laughter of children in the park, or the sound of a distant helicopter, would drag him back to the battlefield. The scars, though less visible now, were still there. They never fully disappeared, and James had learned to accept them as part of his identity.

That morning, as he sat at the kitchen table with Sarah, he realised that he hadn't thought about the war as much lately. It wasn't gone, but it had taken a quieter place in his mind.

"How do you feel about starting a family?" Sarah asked softly, her eyes meeting him across the table.

The question had been lingering between them for months, but today, it felt like the right time.

James took a deep breath. He'd thought about it a lot. He wanted to share his life with her in that way, wanted to build a family. But part of him was scared, scared that he wasn't enough, scared that the shadows of his past would somehow steal that future away from him.

"I'm ready," he said quietly, his voice firm despite the uncertainty that swirled within him. "But I need you to know that there are parts of me… parts of the past that might have come up when I least expected it. I can't promise you I'll be perfect."

Sarah smiled gently, reaching across the table to take his hand. "I don't need you to be perfect, James. I just need you to be you."

It was simple, but it was exactly what he needed to hear. He squeezed her hand, feeling the weight of that unspoken promise. He didn't have to carry everything alone anymore.

James's decision to start a family wasn't an easy one. Even as he and Sarah began discussing their future, his mind drifted back to the soldiers who had fought beside him. His brothers. He had seen how they struggled with their own families, with the weight of fatherhood, with the fear that they might not be able to be the men they wanted to be.

Nathan, who had been married for a few years now, had often shared his doubts with James. "I still hear their voices sometimes," he had said once, his eyes haunted. "I wonder if I'm doing enough for my family when I can't even heal what's inside me."

It was the same feeling James had always carried. The sense that no matter what you did, no matter how much love you gave, the past was always there, a shadow over your shoulder.

But slowly, over time, both James and Nathan had come to realise that they couldn't keep running from their pasts. They had to find ways to integrate it into their lives, to shape the future without letting the past completely define them. They leaned on each other more now than they had in years.

As Sarah and James started planning for their child, he found himself thinking about what kind of father he wanted to be. He wanted to be the kind of father who showed up, who listened, who gave his children the stability and love he hadn't always had. But he also knew that he couldn't escape the things that had shaped him, and he couldn't promise he would never have a bad day.

But that was the point. He didn't have to be perfect. He just had to keep showing up.

The day Sarah told James she was pregnant was one of the happiest moments of his life. She had waited for the right moment to share the news, knowing how much it would mean to him.

The joy he felt was immediate, overwhelming, yet tempered by the quiet understanding that this new life would require him to face a whole new set of challenges. Not just as a soldier, but as a father, as a man who had lived through things that he had to learn to leave behind.

They decided not to find out the gender of the baby. It felt right to leave that part of the journey a mystery, just like everything else they had ahead of them. They would navigate it together, as a family. It was a new beginning, a fresh chapter, and James could feel the hope that it brought bubbling up inside him.

In the months that followed, he began to prepare, not just for the arrival of their child, but for the kind of father he hoped to be. He worked with veterans, helping them transition back into civilian life, and spent time with his old platoon members, reminding himself that they weren't just survivors, they were part of the foundation of who he had become.

There was still so much to learn, so many things he wasn't sure how to handle, but he felt ready.

It wasn't about being perfect, it was about being present, about showing up for his family in the way that mattered most.

One crisp autumn afternoon, James found himself driving down the familiar roads that led to the old cemetery. He hadn't been back in years, not since the reunion. But today, there was a sense of finality, of peace, that pushed him to return.

He parked the car and walked slowly toward the graves. As he passed each stone, each name etched into the cold marble, memories rushed back, faces of men who had been more than soldiers to him. They had been brothers, they had been family.

He stopped in front of Harris's grave first, his heart heavy. He had thought about Harris often over the years. The man had been his rock in the field, the one who always had his back. The one he had failed to save.

"I've been thinking about you a lot," James whispered, kneeling in front of the stone. "I don't know if I'll ever stop.

But I promise I'm doing my best. I'm going to be a father, Harris. And I'm going to do it right. I'll make sure my kid know what it means to survive, to honour the people who didn't get to come home."

He sat there for a long time, letting the stillness settle around him. The grief didn't feel as sharp as it had all those years ago. Instead, it was just a part of him now, like a scar that never quite faded but no longer hurt.

A few months later, Sarah gave birth to their first child, a boy they named Lucas. James couldn't quite describe the feeling of holding him for the first time, the overwhelming mix of love, fear, and responsibility. The world felt new, even though it had always been the same.

He stared down at his son's tiny face, and for the first time in a long time, the weight of the past seemed to lift. Lucas was his future. He was the reason James could finally look ahead without fear.

In the years that followed, James continued to balance the challenges of fatherhood, his work, and his personal journey. He often thought about his brothers in arms, about Nathan, Marco, and the men he had lost. They remained a part of his story, and always would.

But now, he had a new story to live one of hope, of love, of a future that was still unfolding.

And as he looked into his son's eyes, James knew one thing with absolute certainty: he had survived for a reason. The war had taken so much from him, but it had also given him something invaluable: his strength, his resilience, and the people who stood by his side. And now, it had given him a family.

As the years went on, James found himself marvelling at the way Lucas had begun to grow, changing from a helpless infant into a curious, energetic child with a mind of his own. It was humbling, there were times when he couldn't quite believe how quickly the days passed, how quickly his son became more independent, more confident in his own world.

There were moments when James would watch Lucas struggle with something small, tying his shoes, or figuring out how to ride a bike, and he'd feel a rush of pride. It wasn't just in the victories, but in the determination, the willingness to fail and try again. That was something James had seen in himself, something he recognised deeply.

Sarah had become not just a partner in raising their son but a partner in life. They had both healed in ways they hadn't anticipated, finding balance between their pasts and the future they were building together. They learned to lean on each other, to forgive, to share the burdens of parenthood, and, most importantly, to let love take centre stage in their home.

There were hard days, of course. The weight of memories never fully disappeared, and some nights, when the house was quiet and everyone was asleep, James could still feel the echoes of the past. The loss. The anger. The sorrow.

But he'd learned to live with it. He no longer tried to erase those pieces of himself. Instead, he let them exist alongside the joy and hope that Lucas had brought into their lives.

It was a delicate balance, but one he was learning to navigate with grace.

And sometimes, on rare moments when he was alone, James would let his thoughts drift back to his brothers, those he'd lost and those still scattered across the world. They were with him, in the memories they'd shared, in the lessons they'd taught him. It was a strange comfort, knowing that they lived on in him, in the choices he made, in the life he was building.

One evening, as they sat together in the backyard, Lucas ran circles around them, his laughter bright against the backdrop of the setting sun. Sarah smiled, her eyes soft with affection. James caught her gaze and, for a moment, everything else faded away. The future he had feared was now here, unfolding in the most beautiful, unexpected way.

"Look at him," Sarah said, her voice quiet but full of warmth. "He's growing so fast."

James nodded, his heart swelling. "He is. I can't believe how much time has passed."

"He's going to do great things," she added, her smile widening. "He's got so much love and strength in him. Just like his father."

James chuckled softly, feeling the heat of her words. "I don't know about that... but I'll do my best to show him how to be strong."

"You already are," she said, her voice filled with certainty.

James looked at Lucas again, racing around, his face flushed with joy. He had learned so much from this little boy, about resilience, about unconditional love, about the importance of hope. The war had taken so much from him, but it had also shaped him into the father he was now. And it had brought him to this moment, the quiet joy of watching his son, with all his potential, discover the world.

It wasn't just about survival anymore. It was about living. And now, more than ever, James knew that he had everything he needed to make that life one worth living.

As the evening faded into night, with the stars beginning to shimmer above them, James made a silent promise to his son.

He would do whatever it took to protect this life, to guide him, to help him grow into the man he was destined to be.

This was a story that would never end. It was just beginning.

CHAPTER 10 TRANQUILLITY

As the years continued to pass, James found himself looking at life through a different lens. Fatherhood had shifted his priorities. Where once he had focused on the weight of his own survival, now his focus was on nurturing and guiding Lucas through the world.

It was as though the scars of his past had found a place to rest, no longer dictating his every move but rather quietly reminding him of how far he'd come.

Lucas, with his boundless energy and infectious curiosity, was a constant source of inspiration. He asked questions that made James reflect on things he hadn't thought about in years. Why do the stars twinkle? Why do people fight? Why can't everyone be happy all the time?

The questions, simple as they were, often sent James into deep thought. It wasn't always easy to explain the complexity of the world to his young son, but he tried.

He wanted Lucas to grow up knowing that the world wasn't defined solely by hardship, that there was beauty in it too, beauty that could be seen in small moments, in a smile, in a shared laugh, in the way the sunlight caught the leaves on a crisp autumn morning.

It wasn't just the big milestones, first words, first steps, that filled James's heart with pride. There were the quiet moments too. The way Lucas looked at him for reassurance when he was unsure, or the times he would climb into James's lap after a long day, exhausted and seeking comfort. In those moments, James felt his purpose fully aligned. This was what it had all been for, the chance to create a different life for his son. A life filled with love, safety, and the freedom to grow without fear.

Sarah, too, continued to be his anchor. There was a quiet strength in her that James admired. She didn't try to fix everything, didn't try to erase the past. She simply stood beside him, offering her love and her patience when he needed it most.

Their bond deepened as they navigated the rollercoaster of parenthood together, finding joy in the chaos and calm in the unpredictable rhythms of their lives. They didn't have all the answers, but they had each other, and that was more than enough.

And yet, there were moments, those fleeting, quiet moments, when James would find himself alone with his thoughts. The weight of the past still lingered, never fully gone. There were nights when the dreams would come, dark and vivid, pulling him back to places he wished he could forget.

Faces of men he had fought beside, of lives lost and never truly understood. He had learned to carry the grief, to let it be a part of him without letting it consume him. But sometimes, especially in the quiet of the night, he couldn't help but feel the absence of those he had lost.

One evening, after Lucas had gone to bed, James and Sarah sat on the porch together, the night air cool and crisp around them. They were quiet for a while, both content in the shared space, the soft hum of the world around them filling the silence.

"You ever wonder…" Sarah began, her voice gentle, as though testing the waters. "What would Nathan, Marco, and others would think of him?"

James's heart clenched at the mention of their names, but he nodded. "All the time."

"Do you think they'd be proud?"

A small smile tugged at James's lips as he thought about it. "Yeah. I think they would be. They would've loved to see him grow up."

"Me too," Sarah said softly, her gaze turned toward the stars. "They gave us the chance to do this, didn't they?"

James nodded again, his chest tight but full. "They did. And I'll make sure Lucas knows about them. He deserves to know the men who helped us get here."

They sat together in the stillness, each lost in their thoughts, but bound by a quiet understanding. Life was fragile. Time was fleeting. But they had this moment. They had each other. And that, James realised, was enough.

As the years moved on, Lucas began to ask more complex questions, about the past, about his family's history, about the world beyond the home they had built.

James found himself telling Lucas stories, not just of his own life, but of those who had shaped him. Nathan, Marco, the men who had stood by him in the trenches, who had laughed with him in the darkest of times. He spoke of their courage, their loyalty, and the strength they had given him, not as a way to hold onto the past, but as a way to honour it.

"Your dad has been through a lot," James would say, "but it's because of people like Nathan and Marco that we have the chance to make a better world. To live the way we do now."

Lucas would listen, wide eyed, absorbing the stories of the men who had shaped his father. And in those moments, James felt something stir within him, he wasn't just telling Lucas about the past. He was building the foundation for a future, for a legacy that would carry on.

The war had tried to take everything. It had stolen pieces of his soul, pieces of his past, and pieces of those he loved.

But now, looking at Lucas, his son, his future, he understood. The fight hadn't been for nothing.

He had fought to survive, not just for himself, but for the family he had created. For the life he had built. And in that, James found peace. The past could never be erased, but the future, his family, his son, was worth every sacrifice.

And as he watched Lucas grow, he knew the most important lesson of all: it wasn't just about surviving. It was about living.

It was about learning, growing, and giving everything you had to the people you loved. And in that, James had found his reason for everything.

As the years continued to pass, life in the small, quiet house was full of the laughter of children, the warmth of shared moments, and the steady rhythm of everyday life. But James had learned to never take any of it for granted. Time had taught him that nothing was permanent, and the fleeting nature of it all hung over him, especially as Lucas grew older.

There were days when Lucas's questions grew deeper, his thoughts more complex. "Dad," he asked one evening as they were sitting on the porch, watching the sunset, "what was it like when you were in the army?"

The question had come more often recently, as Lucas grew old enough to understand that his father's past was something he hadn't always spoken about. James felt a familiar tightening in his chest. He had been trying to protect his son from the darker parts of his story, but Lucas was growing up. The veil of innocence was slowly lifting, and with it, the weight of history.

James took a deep breath, searching for the right words. "It was hard, son. It was a time full of fear, and loss, and… things I wish I didn't have to see." His voice cracked slightly, the years of buried emotion threatening to resurface. "But I did it because I had to. To protect the people I loved. And because of that, you're here. You and your mom, you're my reason for everything now."

Lucas nodded solemnly, but James could see the questions still lingering in his eyes.

He had always tried to shield him from the worst
of the past, but Lucas was growing up too fast,
and there was only so much he could protect
him from.

And yet, despite the weight of those memories,
life went on. But as the years passed, James
began to notice the changes in his body, the
aches that wouldn't go away, the exhaustion that
seemed to deepen with each passing day. At first,
it was easy to dismiss, everyone got older, right?
But slowly, those little signs became harder to
ignore.

He started missing more and more days of work,
feeling drained, his mind clouded, and his body
protesting at every turn. There were nights when
sleep eluded him, leaving him tossing and
turning, his mind wandering back to places he
could never truly leave behind.

Then came the diagnosis.

It hit like a punch to the gut, a heavy, cold weight
that James could hardly comprehend. Cancer.
Aggressive, advanced. It wasn't something that
could be fought for forever. He had always been
a survivor.

He had survived the horrors of war, the loss of his brothers in arms, the dark nights alone with his thoughts. But, this was different. The strength he had carried with him for so long felt like it was slipping away, leaving him powerless to fight back.

The doctors gave him their best predictions, but nothing could erase the inevitable truth: time was running out. He tried to be strong, to hide his fear from Sarah and Lucas, but there were moments, those quiet, intimate moments when it was just him and his wife, that he couldn't help but break down.

"James," Sarah would whisper, her voice trembling with fear and love, "we'll fight this together. You're not alone."

But how could he explain to her the sinking feeling in his chest? How could he tell her that he felt like his body was betraying him, just as his mind had been scarred so many years ago?

Lucas, ever the curious child, started to ask more questions, asking why his father was always so tired, why he couldn't play catch as much anymore.

James would smile as best as he could, trying to hide the truth. He didn't want to burden his son with the reality of what was happening. He didn't want Lucas to feel the weight of his illness, to grow up with the shadow of loss hanging over him too soon.

And yet, there was no escaping it.

The days began to blur together. The hospital visits, the treatments, the quiet moments at home when James could see the sadness in Sarah's eyes, the way Lucas looked at him with concern that he couldn't quite understand.

The future he had fought so hard to build, his family, his son, the chance to watch Lucas grow, was slipping through his fingers, and no amount of strength or resilience could change that.

There was one evening, months after the diagnosis, when James sat with Lucas in the backyard. The night air was cool, and the sound of crickets filled the surrounding silence. Lucas was trying to master riding his bike without training wheels, but his confidence wavered each time he wobbled. James watched, proud of his son, even in the midst of his own struggle.

"Dad," Lucas said, his voice quiet, "can you teach me how to ride without falling?"

James smiled, though it was a bittersweet one. "You're doing great, buddy. Just keep trying. You'll get it. I know you will."

But there was a hollow ache in James's chest as he watched his son, knowing that the time he had left to teach him, to guide him, was growing shorter with every passing day.

That night, as they sat together on the porch, James wrapped his arm around Sarah, holding her close. She rested her head on his shoulder, her breath shaky. Words were unnecessary. They had both come to understand the truth, they couldn't outrun this. There was no more pretending that everything was okay.

"I'm scared," Sarah whispered, her voice barely audible.

"I know," James replied, his throat tight. "Me too. But we'll make sure Lucas is okay. We'll make sure he knows he's loved. He'll be fine. He's got you."

Sarah squeezed his hand, her tears falling quietly, her heartbreak for the man she loved and the son they had raised together.

And as James lay in bed that night, the pain in his body worsening, the fear of the unknown rising, he thought about his journey, how he had survived the war, how he had survived the darkness of his past, how he had built a future. But now, the hardest part of all lay ahead of him.

He survived for a reason. He had lived for this family, for the chance to create something better. And though the road ahead would be filled with heartache, he would leave behind something beautiful, a legacy of love, of sacrifice, of resilience.

And as the days passed, with his strength fading, James held onto the one thing he could, the knowledge that Lucas and Sarah would be okay, that the love they had built would carry them through the hardest of times.

But in his heart, he couldn't help but ache for all the moments he would miss, the birthdays, the graduations, the first loves, the future he wouldn't be there to see.

As much as he had fought for this life, it was slipping through his fingers, and no matter how hard he fought, there was no way to hold on to it forever.

In the end, James's journey wasn't one of perfect resolution, but of love, loss, and the bittersweet understanding that sometimes, the hardest battles were the ones you couldn't win.

James's health continued to decline, each day feeling like a long, silent march toward something he couldn't escape. His body was growing weaker, his mind increasingly clouded, but through it all, his love for Sarah and Lucas remained his anchor. He held onto them as tightly as he could, trying to shield them from the reality of what was coming, even though they both knew. It was unspoken, but it was there, looming, undeniable.

It became harder to get out of bed, harder to keep up the charade of normalcy for Lucas. He still smiled when Lucas asked him to play, but there was no hiding the exhaustion in his eyes.

No hiding the way he'd stumble when he tried to walk, the way his breath hitched when he exerted himself even a little. It wasn't the way he wanted to go out. He had survived too much to go out like this, silent, fading, helpless.

But this wasn't a battle he could win. He could fight the memories of war, he could survive the grief of losing his comrades, but this was something else entirely.

It wasn't just his body that was failing him; it was everything he had worked for. The family, the love, the future he had dreamed of, he could feel it all slipping through his fingers. And there was nothing he could do to stop it.

One evening, as the sun dipped below the horizon, casting a soft orange glow over the yard, James found himself sitting on the porch with Sarah and Lucas. The cool air was comforting, but it only highlighted the growing emptiness in his chest. Sarah sat beside him, her hand resting on his, her warmth a reminder of everything he was about to lose.

"Dad," Lucas's voice broke through the quiet. "Are you going to be okay?"

James smiled, but it didn't reach his eyes. He wanted so badly to tell Lucas everything would be fine, that he would be there for all of it, the first day of high school, his first job, his wedding. But those moments weren't promised to him. They were promises he couldn't keep.

"I'm going to be okay," he said softly, but the words felt hollow, even to him. He squeezed Lucas's hand, trying to give him the comfort he couldn't fully provide. "But there's something I need you to know.

You're strong. And no matter what happens, you'll always have your mom. And you'll always have me, here, in your heart."

Lucas, his face full of confusion and sadness, nodded but didn't say anything more. James could see the weight of the truth settling on him, but there was nothing he could do to ease it. He wasn't ready to face the loss of his father, no child ever was.

As the days passed, the small moments of joy they had shared started to feel more like precious, fleeting memories. The days of laughter, of teaching Lucas to ride his bike, of playing games together in the yard, seemed to slip away as quickly as the seasons changed. James had always thought that by fighting through the hardest times, he could protect the people he loved. But now, he realised that no amount of strength or willpower could stop time, could stop the inevitable.

One afternoon, Sarah found him sitting by the window, staring out at the yard, watching Lucas run around with his friends. His body was frail now, the disease taking what little strength remained. The man who had once been strong enough to survive everything was now unable to lift his own weight. And yet, at that moment, as he watched Lucas play, there was peace in him.

It wasn't the peace of knowing that everything would turn out all right. It was the peace of knowing that, at least for a time, he had done everything he could.

"I'm sorry," James whispered, his voice barely audible, his hand still holding Sarah's tightly. "I'm sorry I won't be here for him."

Sarah leaned into him, her tears falling silently, a mixture of love and sorrow. "You've already given him everything, James. You've given him more than you'll ever know."

But it wasn't enough for him. He wanted more. He wanted to be there for Lucas's first heartbreak, his first big decision, his life as an adult. He wanted to be there when Lucas became a man, and wanted to see the person he would become.

But as the days turned to weeks, and the weeks turned to months, it became clear that time was slipping away. The pain was sharper now, his body growing weaker, and the moments with his family more precious than ever. Lucas didn't fully understand the gravity of the situation, but he knew something was wrong. The smile he once saw on his father's face had faded, and the laughter they shared had become less frequent.

There was one final night, just a few days before James's strength failed him completely, when Sarah and Lucas sat beside him, holding his hand.

The room was quiet, filled with the soft hum of the world outside, and for a moment, James felt as though everything had come full circle. He wasn't the man he had been in the war, broken, haunted by the past.

He had rebuilt himself, found a reason to live in the face of the horrors that had once consumed him. But now, as he lay there in the dim light, he realised that no matter how hard he tried, he couldn't outlast this fight.

"Lucas," James whispered, his voice weak but filled with love. "Take care of your mom. Always protect her. And you know… you're everything I ever wanted. You're my legacy."

Lucas squeezed his hand, tears in his eyes, not yet able to fully grasp the meaning of his father's words. "I love you, Dad."

"I love you too, son," James said, his voice barely a breath, a tear slipping down his cheek as he looked at his family. "I'll always be with you."

And as the light dimmed, and the final breath escaped his chest, James felt a quiet peace. He hadn't won every battle. He hadn't been there for every moment he had dreamed of. But he had fought with everything he had. And he had loved, loved deeper than he ever thought possible.

His journey had been full of heartache, but it had also been full of love. And in the end, love was the only thing that truly remained.

James's story ended, but the legacy he had created with Sarah and Lucas would live on. It would live on in every step Lucas took, in every lesson he carried forward, and in the love that would continue to bind their family together, even after his absence.

The End!!!

Printed in Dunstable, United Kingdom